Broken Earth

Broken Earth Copyright © 2013 Lee Ryder

Cover by Sprinkles on Top Studios

Published By Ryder Publishing

Edited by: Judy Steinberg-Cainaru

All rights reserved. In accordance with the U.S. Copyright Act of 1976, the scanning, uploading, and electronic sharing of this book without the permission of the publisher constitute unlawful piracy and theft of the author's intellectual property. If you would like to use material from the book (other than for review purposes), permission must be obtained by contacting the publisher. We appreciate your support of the author's rights.

The characters and events in this book are fictitious. Any similarity to real persons, living or dead is coincidental and not intended by the author.

Author's Note

Thank you *God* for all the gifts you have given me every day!

Sprinkles on Top Studios for my amazing book cover!

Becki Brannen for teaching me the ropes of publishing my own book, you are amazing.

Thank you to my amazing mother in law Judy for editing this for me.

Thank you to the amazing RaeBeth Buda for all her help with editing and formatting.

My dear friend Christy for helping me get where I needed to be to be able to put this all together thank you for your patience and advice.

There are so many people I want to thank for making this book happen, All the people that stand behind me and beside me are so special. I love each one of them.

Thank you to the MTT Girls Kellie M, Heather S, Nanette you guys rock!

My husband and children for giving me the endless love and energy I needed to be able to write this book. My writing cave is loud and full of love.

Thank you Mom and Dad for always believing in me, for sharing your wisdom and your encouragement. You inspire me every day with your never-ending love and compassion for others. You always have been there for me. I don't know where I'd be without you. I love you SO much.

My beautiful and loving brothers and sisters there are so many things I can say but none of it would begin to touch how much I love you.

Thank you to my Tributes ladies Becki, Robin, Julie, and Joyce. My Twilight sisters whose positivity and love keep me going every day Kellie, Candice, Angie, RaeBeth, Tianna, Celsie, Aileen, Lisa, all the TCML Lubs and Twi-Mom Faebook ladies, and so many more.

My Lord of Life and Town Line Lutheran families for helping me keep my faith even in my darkest times.

"The earth is utterly broken down, the earth is clean dissolved, and the earth is moved exceedingly.

Isaiah 24:19

What has gone before…

It all began with a war. It was not between countries, or even Heaven and Earth, but between humans and the earth. It started over a thousand years ago when our ancestors began using the Earth's resources for industry. The industrial machine craved natural resources for centuries, which slowly depleted natural resources. The result caused humans to become more reliant on new resources. Then, once again, the resources would be depleted. This cycle repeated, which set us where we are today. The skies became darkened with soot and a layer covers everything. Every day we had to clean the soot off our bodies to try to stop it from choking us. We washed in the morning, midday, and in the evening to remain relatively healthy. It was an endless cycle, even now with all the industries shut down.

The parks were destroyed to make room for factories. The Grand Canyon was filled in and turned into an industrial center, which made weapons to strengthen the power of the governments. Governments fought against each other for a stronger foothold in the common market. The governments would increase prices daily because pressures put on them by big industry. There were not any regulations on producers; they ruthlessly poisoned the environment with their toxic waste. The rich got richer and the poor worked harder.

Suddenly, people began to die. It was a few at first. Their lives were claimed by cancer, black lung, and heart diseases. The pollution in the air from the factories and mines clouded the skies, and made everyone sick. The governments did nothing; their only focus was on their never-ending quest for more money.

Then, the plagues started. People died from tuberculosis, AIDS, scarlet fever, bubonic plague, the flu, and another unknown wasting disease. The feared wasting disease was so virulent that mass graveyards grew in the rural areas surrounding the cities. In order to make room for the growing need to bury the dead, buildings had to be torn down, and the earth beneath them broken as people began to die en masse.

The death industry began to grow. The rich paid for lavish funerals and huge, ornately carved, white marble mausoleums that were quickly turned gray by the soot like everything else. They stood as a reminder of what the world has become, an ironic joke marking the skyline of a world that has met its end of days.

The trees became barren, and the world was devoid of the life, which once occupied the vast wooded areas that were once forests and parks. The cities turned into ghost towns. Those who lived there exist on meals of rats one day, and boiled bugs the next. Those that were lucky would find a mushroom or two at the edges of the city in the graveyards. Unfortunately, most people believed that if you ate them, death would follow.

I was one of the lucky ones who were seemingly immune to the spreading disease. Lucky, yeah…right. My entire family died. After my father was killed in an accident while working at the steelworks, my mother, brother, and sister were taken from me by the wasting disease. I remained in our apartment, while I sold off anything, which was not nailed down, to be able to survive. As the people died, the looting began. I was as guilty as the others were, but if it meant that I could survive, no one could condemn me. I picked up the soot-smudged picture of my family, and used my dingy shirt to clean the glass. They smiled up at me, which reminded me of better days when the air was clean, the water pure, and on a good day, you could still see a little blue in the sky.

I sighed and put the picture back down beside my makeshift bed, which consisted of a dingy sleeping bag and a pillow made of relatively clean rags. They were the first faces I saw in the day and the last I saw as I fell exhausted onto my pillow at night.

Chapter 1

Early in the morning, loud pounding on my door wakes me up. I scramble to my feet and grab my crossbow, hoping to Heaven that it's not one of the many street gangs that had been robbing and looting in the city the night before.

"Jess wake up!" Ian calls through the door, while banging on it.

"I'm coming!" I yell back, irritated because the pounding woke me out of a pseudo peaceful slumber.

As he saunters in, I aim my crossbow directly at his heart.

"I surrender!" He says, while he eyes my crossbow, and winks at me.

"What the heck are you doing here so early?" I ask walking over to the cabinet where I have stashed away a few mushrooms. (I never bought into the whole death superstition following the graveyard mushrooms.)

I tossed one to Ian; he catches and promptly drops it on the floor wiping his hands frantically on his pants. "*Superstitious idiot*" I thought, as I try to quell a giggle.

We sit down on my sleeping bag and get comfortable as Ian eyes me eating my mushroom.

"What are you staring at?" I ask.

"Nothing, I'm just watching to see if anything happens." He answers with a smirk on his face, his green eyes twinkling at me.

I punch him playfully in the arm. "So, what are you doing here so early?"

His face grows somber, and he pulls his hand through his tangled brown curls. "Justilian was killed last night in his apartment. I went to check on him, and it looked as if he was raided by one of the gangs."

Justilian was one of the oldest inhabitants of the apartment building we lived in. He was twenty-three, and had been working as an engineer in the city before everyone died. The offices, stores, businesses, and industrial centers were closed up. The gangs rounded up workers, so they could produce the things they knew people would need. You paid dearly in favors, food, or work, for these items unless you traded on the black market for them. However, either way you still paid dearly. Overall, none of the survivors wanted to owe their lives to the gangs.

"How do you know it was one of the gangs?" I asked, wiping my hands on my pants.

"Well, his apartment was tagged, and they took his entire supply of PDQ." Ian said, shaking his head.

PDQ was a nutritional supplement with the consistency of baby food, which was intended to act as a meal replacement. The Government developed it when the food stores were depleted. PDQ is meant to give you a half a day's supply of nutrients one needs. It allows one to work effectively in the factories without being worn out from the lack of the daily nutrients needed. The daily ration of PDQ was two bottles and that was what you were expected to live on each day. The downside of this stuff is there is a potent stimulant in it, which is meant to keep people going so they did not think about food. The gangs found a way of extracting this stimulant while using it to keep people addicted. This way they would work to build the gangs' supply storehouses. They would be forced to do hard labor just to get a pittance of the supplies they needed.

Justilian had been using the PDQ for a different purpose he found there was a medicinal quality to it if used correctly. He would go through the city helping sick and starving kids. Sometimes, Ian and I would help him take care of the youngest plague survivors. We would find them and take them to safe houses Justilian set up with older survivors. The younger ones worked together to learn the skills they needed in order to survive.

"Did they take anything else?" I asked him in disbelief.

"No, just the PDQ and some food, I think the gang who did it knew he had it. It wasn't random." He answered shaking his head. "He was probably being watched.

"Do you know who it was?"

"The tag on his wall looks like the one the Stingers had been using, but I can't be sure." Ian answered. "What are the survivors going to do without Justilian?"

"We'll have to take over where he left off. That's all we can do."

"We don't have the supplies or the knowledge he had." Ian said angrily.

"Well, we can't do anything just sitting here." I said standing up, and offering Ian my hand. "We need to go to his apartment and see what we can find there. Then, I said quietly, "We also need to bury Justilian."

"Bury him?" Ian asks, as he looks at me nervously, unconsciously dropping my hand. In his sixteen years, he only buried one other person, his brother.

Ian never talked about his family. He only talked about his older brother. There was a lot of mystery in Ian's life. I hoped that one day he would be comfortable enough to tell me where his family had been before the plagues.

"Yes, bury him; he would do the same for us." I said a little irritated that this big strong sixteen-year-old man couldn't stomach burying one of our closest friends.

"All right" Ian said, taking my hand.

I pull him to his feet, and then grab my pack and crossbow just in case we need it.

"Do you want to stop at your apartment and tell Lucie where we're going?"

"We probably should. She'll freak out if she hears about Justilian from anyone but me." Ian agreed.

Lucie was Ian's seven-year-old sister, she had beautiful blonde hair and pretty blue eyes. She reminded me a lot of my sister McKenna when she was not sick. I had a soft spot for this little girl and Ian knew it. He knew if he crossed her at all, he would have me to answer to, and it would not be pretty!

Lucie met us at the apartment door. I knew he was in trouble.

"Ian, where have you been?" Lucie demanded, hitting her older brother in the chest with her tiny fist. "I was so afraid when I woke up and you were gone! I thought you were taken by one of the gangs!"

"Take it easy stinky!" He said feigning defeat. "I was just visiting Jess!"

I stifled a laugh at the banter between Lucie and Ian.

"Hey Luce," I said, smiling down at her and ruffling her hair. "I need you to do me a favor."

"What kind of a favor?" Lucie says smiling at me wistfully. Ian told me she completely idolized me.

"I need you to stay inside this apartment with this door locked until we get back. Can you do that?" I say, as I kneel in front of her so I can look into her eyes.

"By myself?" She asks nervously. She is terrified of the gangs, and of everything that goes on outside of the apartment walls. Ian has never taken her out. Little girls like her were often taken then sold into slavery, and sometimes forced to do even more unspeakable things.

"Yes, you're going to be fine. Ian and I need to do something. Okay?"

Lucie began to giggle. "Are you gonna go kiss?" She asked.

Ian burst out laughing. "Kiss Jess? Are you crazy?"

A lump forms in my throat, I know it's a joke, but it still hurts.

I had a crush on Ian for a long time, since he moved here.

"No," I murmur. "We have to go out for supplies. You know those things we get so we don't starve?"

Lucie giggled again.

"So, Luce, you're gonna stay here right?" Ian asks quickly, changing the subject.

"We'll be back before you can miss us." I said reassuringly, and smiled at her. This brought on another wave of giggles.

Ian walked by Lucie into the apartment ruffling her pretty, blonde curls on his way past. She watched him nervously, as he loaded his pack and came back to the door.

"Are you sure you both have to go?" She asks, as nervousness creeps back into her voice.

"Lock the door Luce. I promise I'll be back." Ian said, kissing her on the forehead and giving her a reassuring hug.

"I promise." I say to her, putting my hand on her shoulder and giving it a quick squeeze. "You're a tough girl, right?"

"Right," she answers not quite believing it herself.

Chapter 2

When we got to Justilian's apartment, it was eerily quiet. Normally, Justilian was out in the hallway feeding the survivors who lived in the building, along with any other people who showed up at the door. He had a tremendous love for the world, and everyone in it. He was so trusting, sometimes too trusting. This time his trusting nature got the better of him, and got him killed.

I gently pushed the door open; nothing seemed out of place. We saw that everything had been ransacked. They were looking for one thing, P.D.Q. DAMN THEM! I made a mental note to come back and clean this up. Now his apartment will be a shrine to the amazing person he was.

Justilian's body was on the floor in his living room. His beautiful glass table was shattered into a million pieces. Justilian was so proud of that table. He found it in the trash and fixed it by himself using bits and pieces of glass pieces he found around the neighborhood. The table was truly a work of art with its gorgeous stained glass effect. He kept it clean and polished. He believed that this one small table made the world seem a little bit more civilized. It was a little piece of what we all had before, something that was still beautiful, untouched by the ugliness around us. A poignant reminder that we could rebuild our world and that nothing had to stay broken. It could be restored, and be made beautiful again. It brought him hope.

I went to Justilian's room and got a clean blanket to cover his body. Ian helped me wrap the blanket around him so we could get him to my cart. I really do not want people to stare. He would be another nameless body needing to be buried. I didn't want to think about it right now.

If he didn't have the cut on his head, it would look like he was sleeping. He could have opened his eyes any moment and given me that bright smile which, always warmed my heart and reminded me I was not alone in this world. The one, which always said, "You're important to me. You're special."

"I'm so sorry this happened to you." I whispered, kissing him on the forehead, while a lump forms in my throat. I choke back my tears, because I know he is free.

I stroke his hair and kiss his forehead again, as he would always kiss mine when I left his home to go back to my apartment. He was like an older brother to me. I will miss his mischievous grin, rumbling laugh, and the sparkle in his eyes when he would greet me. He was always so happy to have me visit him and spend time with him. Now, I was alone again.

I finger the bible in my pocket. I brought it so I could read a verse or two as we bury him.

My mother always said, "Everyone deserves a good Christian burial."

I will not deny this to Justilian. He was as Christian as they came. He prayed over the sick and dying. He buried his friends, and his enemies, without prejudice. He had such a good soul and it made no sense to me why he left this earth too soon. He had more good things to do, or at least I thought so.

I bent to kiss him again, "Goodnight my sweet prince." I whisper to him.

We bury Justilian in the furthest corner of the cemetery, which is next to many of the city's founders. We had to be careful when we buried someone here, because there were so many unmarked graves, and it is believed that you would be cursed if you disturbed one. I, of course, do not believe it, but one can never be too careful. I will make sure to come back later and make a fitting marker for him.

"He was the best of us." Ian chokes wiping at the tears on his face futilely with his dirty hands. "Without him Lucie would have died last winter."

I nod in agreement. Justilian got the antibiotics that saved Lucie's life. She had contracted pneumonia last winter from the bitter cold in our building, and we all thought she was going to die.

Justilian had to trek to the middle of the city where the old hospital was. It was an area held under the thumb of a particularly nasty gang called the Razorbacks. Their leader was a masochistic and frightening eighteen-year-old boy called Ash, but his gang called him Rebel. I knew him when we were in school, and he was of course the school bully. He was much larger than many of the other kids and wielded his size like a sword. He was the king of the playground, and whatever he wanted, he took. Everyone feared him and his group of bullies who control the center of the city. You had to be incredibly brave or stupid to go into their territory uninvited and unannounced.

I do not know how Justilian managed to do it, but he really had a way with people to get whatever he needed, whenever he needed it. He was like this Yoda like tribal elder. No one feared him. He was well respected among many of the survivors, and even some of the gangs.

"Jess?" Ian said, waking me from my reverie.

"Yeah?"

"We better get back, or Lucie will start freaking out.

I nod in agreement. Then, kneel down on the freshly dug earth, which covers the body of my friend, my mentor, and my brother. "Until we meet again," I whisper kissing my fingers, and touching them to the earth. "I promise I will keep going and I will try to make the world better where I can. I will make you proud of me."

Ian helps me up, and I dust myself off. I look down at the new grave. It looks so forlorn, so sad. The world lost a bright light, now he knew only darkness.

"How are you going to keep his work going?" Ian asks.

"I don't know yet, but I know we can do it. Together we can do anything."

"Well, that sounds like a sappy movie." Ian said, drolly.

I punch him in the arm. "Sappy is my middle name!"

"Come on." Ian said, "Let's get going before Lucie has a coronary."

I laugh knowing how bad Lucie's melodrama could get, She's a typical seven year old, and I can remember how I was when I was her age, everything was the end of the world.

Chapter 3

I can tell Lucie is relieved when we get back to Ian's apartment. She tries to play it off, and put on a brave front, but I can see right through it. Lucie was still an innocent little girl. I hope that it will never change for her.

I leave Ian to deal with the nine million questions Lucie is bound to have. She's never been further than the front door, due to the danger that lurks in the streets. Ian traveling to the cemetery was big news for her.

I can hear her all the way in the hallway talking excitedly.

"What did the cemetery look like, was it creepy? Did you read any gravestones? Were there a lot of them? Can you draw me a picture?"

"Lucie let me put my backpack down!" Ian exclaims.

I chuckle as I walk out the door, and into the hallway unnoticed by either of them. I head towards my apartment. I will leave breaking the news about Justilian's death to Ian. I was sure she would be very upset. Justilian was one of Lucie's favorite people.

I change direction and go back to Justilian's apartment. I pull out the key that I had taken from his pack and use it to open up the antiquated padlock he kept on his door. He always said that those locks were unbreakable, and he swore by them. He was looking for one to put on my door.

"To keep the boys out." He had teased.

Walking into his apartment without him there is like walking into a mausoleum. I shiver from the cold. The warmth Justilian shared with all who entered his home is gone. It feels like a candle has been snuffed out. When he was there his laughter rang through the walls, and I was sure everyone could hear him. Now there is just an unearthly stillness. I knew he would never truly be at peace.

Slowly, I move through his apartment, taking any necessary items I find, like food and medicine. Oddly enough, I find a good bit stashed away under a floorboard in one of the back bedrooms. I look for anything that I can trade at the marketplace for usable items. I find Justilian's journals. They have to be secreted away within a niche in the floorboards of my apartment where I keep all the things that are important to me. I do not want anyone to get their hands on them. They contain important information on his resources. In the back, he has lists of the people he trades with. He used these resources to help others, and those people definitely needed anonymity. I pack up all the supplies I found into his big army backpack and into a large beat up black suitcases, which I found in one of the back rooms. I put his journals in my small pack to read later. Everything else in the apartment I plan to share with Ian. This time it is not looting. It's survival, and I know Justilian would've done the same thing if something happened to me. On the way out of his apartment, I take a few pictures of Justilian and his family for the remembrance wall at the entrance of the building.

After I leave the two packs and the suitcase in my apartment, I lock the door behind me, so I can go to the remembrance wall.

The wall is nothing fancy, just a large corkboard that used to bear bulletins and notices in the plague days. They put up the daily schedule of when the physicians would visit the building. You could find out where to meet them, or if there were any new immunizations that were being given and where to get them.

After the adults died, the survivors started putting pictures of their families on it. So many survivors are afraid to go into the cemeteries; it gives them a place to remember their friends and loved ones.

I haven't put my family's picture up because, to me, it makes it too permanent. I mean I could have, but for me it just felt hollow. Even putting Justilian's picture here seems wrong. It seems wrong not to. He was a father figure to so many survivors in our building. It seems wrong not to allow them to have a place where they could pay homage to him.

    I move a few pictures over to make room for Justilian's. I want to make sure to put him right in the center of the board so everyone will see his smiling face. I kiss my fingers and touch it to the picture before turning away with tears stinging my eyes.

Chapter 4

The next day Ian and I go through, and split everything left in Justilian's apartment. Then I go back to my apartment to get the things that I'd collected for trading. With Justilian's death, I did not really realize how far behind I am in my trading, and my food store is running low. I am down to a few cans of beans and some graveyard mushrooms.

After checking and re-checking the locks on my door, I head down the dark passageways of the apartments and out into the orange-red daylight.

The trek to the Trader's Den is a very short, but dangerous trip. Two rival gangs, the Flames and the Necromancers are warring and vying for control of the long block of tenement housing that I live in. Everyone who had family members with the wasting disease was sequestered in these tenements, in a failed attempt to try to isolate the disease. The disease mutated and became more virulent than ever. The inevitable squalor brought rodents, and they spread disease much like the 'Black Death' of the dark ages I had learned about in school.

I keep my eyes moving as I pass through the open streets. There are so many different tags on the walls of the buildings from rival gangs trying to claim their territories. Some of them have several layers of tags. I walk faster, because I do not want to become a "mark" for either one of the gangs. Even though I cannot see them, I can feel their eyes on me; and it sends chills down my spine.

The Trader's Den is a "flea market" of sorts. It is located in a burned out grocery store about five blocks from my apartment. My mother sent me there often for food and supplies, before she died from the wasting disease. She always seemed to have the right thing to trade, and knew many of the traders by name.

Today is like any other day at the Trader's Den, extremely busy. It is filled with survivors trading both at booths and in the walkways. I can smell the stench of people, the distinct coppery, salty smell that unwashed flesh gives off. Many of the traders here live right in the den, so their access to 'luxuries' like running water and electricity are extremely limited. The scent here used to make me ill. But, I've been here so often that I've become immune to it.

I know how to maneuver through the maze of walkways and passageways rather quickly to get what I want, and I know who will give me a fair trade. After I get all I think I need, I navigate my way through a short passage and find myself staring into the white coated blind eyes of Mollie.

Mollie is a purveyor of information, and of root vegetables. I am hoping I can trade for both. She is a very good friend and confidante.

"Hi Mollie," I say brightly.

"Nice to see you Jess!" Mollie says in her thick Irish brogue, shaking beautiful thick red curls, which spills over her shoulders as she pulls me into a hug.

Mollie was very young when the virus hit. She contracted a rare form of the disease, but the doctors were able to cure it. The aggressive treatments left Mollie blind, however it was the only reminding piece of her illness. A strange milky white film had formed over her corneas. It made her eyes a haunting translucent blue; and for those who did not know her, that could prove to be a little scary.

"I found this for you." I said, handing her an ornately beaded broach I found in Justilian's apartment. I thought it would be perfect for Mollie, because she could run her fingers over the intricate pattern and "see" it.

"It's blue and white around the outside, with a pretty yellow flower in the middle." I said describing it for her.

A smile lit up Mollie's round face raising her smatter of freckles up towards her eyes and her little nose wrinkles just the tiniest bit.

"A fine gift, a fine gift indeed, thank you!" She said patting my hand. "So what brings you to the gates of Hell?"

I chuckle lightly. "I'm hoping to score some carrots to improve my eyesight." I said using the code words, which meant. "I'm looking for some information."

The gangs have eyes and ears everywhere, so speaking in code was the accepted language of the Trader's Den. There were codes for everything from information, to drugs, to PDQ. The codes change daily, as the gangs got wiser to what people were really talking about.

"Ahh, I'll see what I have." Mollie said, reaching under the counter. "I don't seem to have any right now, but if you would like I will bring some from my garden this evening."

"Good, then I'll make us something to eat." I agree code speak for she will bring the required information later after checking her contacts.

"Are you looking for large or small carrots?" She asked.

"Large ones, they're Justilian's favorite."

"Great! I will bring the largest ones I have!" Mollie agrees, smiling at me widely.

"I will see you for dinner this evening then. You know where I live." I reply giving Mollie a quick hug and heading back to my apartment.

I finish my business at the Trader's Den. Shortly after, I return to my apartment with a small bag of apples, and some tiny wild strawberries. I plan to give Lucie some, because they are her favorite. When I get back, I leave a note on Ian's door to come over for dinner, so he can talk with Mollie as well.

The sky is an orangish black when Ian knocks on my door.

"Is she here yet?" He asks anxiously, while looking around quickly to see if he was followed

"No, not yet, would you please help me get these candles lit?" I answer handing him a Popsicle stick from the box on my counter.

"Wow, do you remember Popsicles?" He asks turning the stick in his fingers. "I used to love the blue ones. I ate all of them out of the package and Luce would get so mad!"

"Yeah, my brother Andrew loved popsicles. He enjoyed the Bomb pops. You know...the one with three flavors. My mom would constantly bribe him with them, so he did his chores." I answers casting a look at the picture of my family on the floor next to my sleeping bag.

I quickly wipe a tear from my eye.

"Hey, what are we eating?" Ian asks nonchalantly not letting on that he had seen my tears.

"Mushroom stew." I answer teasingly, "fresh from the graveyard."

"You have got to be kidding me," he answers wryly, while throwing me a dirty look.

"No, I got some cabbage and a couple tins of Spam. I made a soup out of it."

"Spam and cabbage, how Irish of you." He quipped.

"Shut up and light the candles." I said, punching him in the shoulder.

He stuck his tongue out at me.

"Hey Jess."

"Yeah?"

"I've been hearing about these settlements out west in Utah and Wyoming that have become completely garden societies. The kid who told me said there is so much more food to eat out there. They trade it with the poorer cities around them."

I looked at him. "Really? They've been able to grow things out there?"

"Apparently the sky out there is clearing! Jess, we could go there!" he said taking my hands in his. "Just think; no more gangs, no more cemeteries, and no more starving!"

"It's a fairy tale." I said, shrugging and pulling away from him. "If this place is so good, why doesn't everyone go there?"

"Probably because everyone thinks like you do! That everywhere you go within this country is just like it is here."

"Isn't there?" I spat. "Look what happened, they moved all of us into cities, and walled us into tenements when people got sick. They left us here to die. We had to bury our own people because the adults were dying off and their surviving family members did not have the money to bury their families. They took them to the cemeteries in the dead of night to bury them. This way they wouldn't be arrested for not using a death dealer! Where was the wonderful 'government' of ours when the food ran out? Where were they when the gangs took over?" My voice began to break. "Where were they when my family died, and left me here alone?"

I fell to my knees weeping into my hands. Instantly, I felt Ian's warm arms around me.

"I know Jess, I know." He soothes He picks up my chin so he can look directly into my eyes.

"As long as I am here, you will never be alone. Don't you know that Jess…. I love you."

His words woke something inside of me. Perhaps, it is a want or a need. I needed to believe him, and needed to be with him. He bends to kiss me gently on the lips. I kiss him back; putting everything, I have into it. My pain, my anguish, my loneliness, my entire soul. As we part, I look into his beautiful blue eyes. Had they always been this blue? Like two shining pools of clear water. I see tears running down his cheeks. Were they tears of joy or sadness?

Suddenly, two gentle taps sounded at the door, which are followed after a pause with three more taps. Mollie is here.

Chapter 5

I help Mollie take off the hand-quilted jacket, she made from rags gathered at the trader's den. It is beautifully crafted, and I often wonder how she did it without her sight. She seems to have this sixth sense as to how things should be. She could 'see' things others could not. Many of the gang members fear her and call her a 'witch.' They make certain to give her a wide berth when they meet her.

"Was your trip here safe?" Ian asked, taking Mollie by the elbow, while leading her into the house and around the stored items; I have in what was once the kitchen.

"Aye, me reputation has served me very well. People believe that one look will cause them to have the wasting disease. I guess me eyes are me tickets to safe passage round ere." Mollie says with a huge smile.

"Well, I for one am glad you're on our side." Ian said, pulling a chair into the living area, and leading Mollie to it. He takes her long walking stick, and place it beside her.

Mollie crosses her legs, as I bring her a bowl of the cabbage and spam soup. "It's not much." I say, apologetically.

"It's a feast fit for a king!" Mollie said, raising her bowl in a toast. Nothing ever brings Mollie down.

"So Mollie," Ian says between mouthfuls. "Jess and I were talking about farming settlements out west. I heard there are no gangs and that you can have a peaceful life there, plus there's lots of food."

"Really?" Mollie says, raising a bright red eyebrow.

"Jess said it's just a fairytale. What do you think?" Ian asks.

"I've also e'rd about dis." Mollie said. "T'would be a great place to start over away from dis stinkin city. If I could travel dere meself I would."

"But, do you know if it's real?" I ask.

"I won't say yea, but I would also not say nay either." Mollie answered. "The only sure way to know is to go."

"See" Ian said pointing his spoon at me. "Even Mollie agrees."

"She didn't confirm it!" I shot back.

Mollie's laughter echoes through the empty rooms of my apartment. "You two fight like an old married couple. You remind me of me mum and me da always bickerin about somethin' over dinner."

Ian smiles at me sheepishly in the candlelight. I swear I can see a blush in his cheeks as he looks at me in the firelight.

"Mollie, did you find out anything about Justilian?" I asked, as the tone of the conversation turns somber.

Mollie pauses for a moment, thoughtfully stirring her soup. "He was a good one."

"One of the best." Ian agrees.

I pick up my glass of water, "to Justilian; a friend, a brother, and a survivor."

"To Justilian," Ian and Mollie says, raising their glasses in a salute to our fallen comrade.

After a reverent pause, Mollie puts down her water, and drains the broth from her bowl. I take it from her and collect Ian's bowl from him. I head to the kitchen to place the bowls in the sink. Then, I kneel beside Ian at Mollie's feet.

"Word as' it the Demons got a new shipment of PDQ." Mollie said in a hushed voice.

"From Justilian?" Ian whispers back.

"I'm not sure, but word as' it that Justilian's been bein' watched by both the Nighthawks and the Demons."

"They knew about his PDQ stash?" I ask

"Aye." Mollie confirms. "Although, they didn't know where e' got it."

"No one did." Ian adds.

"So, do you know which gang it was?" I press. "That killed Justilian?"

"Cameron from the Demons came to see me a few weeks ago askin' about Justilian's whereabouts, and where e' lived." Mollie said.

"You didn't tell him did you?" I ask, in shock that a gang member would come within ten feet of Mollie, let alone talk to her.

"No, I'd never do that." Mollie said. "I ad' too much respect for 'J' to do that. He was elpin' so many survivors, including meself. I would never endanger his life. But I did warn

Justilian to be careful, and let him know that e' was bein' watched."

"What! He knew?" I gasp.

"Yes, but that didn't stop him from doing the work e' felt was important. E' knew e' was the only hope that some of these people had." Mollie says, while pointing at us.

"And it cost him his life." I say, shaking my head sadly.

"Aye." Mollie said. "But 'J' believed that the whole was so much more important that 'imself, what e' had e' shared."

"He always did." Ian agrees. "That's just how he was."

"Now darlin' I must be goin." Mollie says, rising to her feet, and reaching back to grab her walking stick. "The hour is late, and the streets are no less forgiving."

She adjusts her beautifully hued, long blue gauzy skirt, and let it unfurl around her. It adds to her mystique.

"Do you want me to walk you home?" Ian offers.

"No sweetheart, me eyes be my protection. No one wants the wastin' disease now do they?" Mollie says, smiling at him.

"Are you sure?" I ask. "With all the fighting, they may do something to you."

"Darlins' I'll be fine." Mollie said reassuringly. I help her on with her coat. "Besides Ian, don't ya have a sister to be tendin' to?"

"Yes." Ian agrees blushing. "Take care Mollie."

"You don't forget where I am!" Mollie replies, shaking her walking stick at us. "You both come down and visit me."

"We sure will Mollie." I say, hugging her. She is family to me. Not only would I visit her, but I would care for her and protect her with my life.

Chapter 6

I watch Ian walk Mollie to the stairs that leads from the second floor of the apartment building to the first floor. He waves at me before opening the door to his apartment, and disappears inside. I am sure Lucie isn't sleeping.

I close my door making sure all the locks are in place, and then begin to clean up the dinner mess. As I collect the rest of the dishes and put them into the sink, I hum *"Amazing Grace"* to myself. It was something my mother did when she was doing the dishes in the evening after our meal, and it makes me feel as if she is still here with me. My mother was always a woman of faith, and kept a Bible on her nightstand. I keep that bible and a few other treasures hidden under my pillow.

I was glad that we still had electricity, but I prefer the more reliable, and inexpensive candles. In order to get light bulbs you need to do a great deal of creative trading, because they have become very rare in the marketplace. My refrigerator is old, but it holds the cold well, as long as it's not opened too many times.

I hear a familiar rap at the door two knocks a pause, and then three knocks. It was a code used by the survivors to indicate a friend was at your door.

"Jess, open up it's me." Ian says quietly.

I open the door. "Is everything okay?"

"Yes, I checked on Luce and she's sleeping, so I thought I would come and help you clean up." He replies.

"Thanks!" I answer, allowing him into the entryway. "I wanted to give you some soup for Luce anyway."

We cleanup the dinner mess while laughing and joking. The spirit is light and comfortable. It always is this way with Ian. He's like cool water refreshing my spirit, and washing away my fears. His gentle touch unwinds my tattered nerves, and his presence calms my soul.

When we were done, I walk him to the door, pausing as he grabbed his shoes. As he stands up, he takes me in his arms and kisses me gently on the cheek. Then brushes another gentle kiss across my lips.

"Good night, beautiful." He says, before he quickly disappears down the hall.

I breathlessly close the door behind me. I can't believe he kissed me again. With a happy heart, I lay out the new sleeping bag and pillow I found in Justilian's apartment. I would be sleeping comfortably tonight.

"Thank you." I whisper looking up.

I blew out all but the two candles nearest to my place on the floor, when again I hear the knocking code on the door.

"What'd you forget?" I say smiling and opening the door.

Suddenly, I am rushed by three dark and very strong figures. Two of them grab my arms and pin me to the floor, while the other straddles me.

"What did you and the witch talk about?" He hisses through his ski mask, his green eyes glittering evilly above me.

"Nothing, she was bringing me vegetables." I lie, trying to be brave.

"That's a LIE!" He growls in a harsh whisper leaning over, and put his hands down on either side of my head, so he can hover very close to my face. His fetid breath is hot on my cheeks; bile churns in my stomach.

"Now, I will ask you once again." He seethes, "what were you and the witch talking about?"

"Nothing!" I scream trying to push myself up futilely.

He slaps me, hard. I can taste blood in my mouth, but I don't cry out. If I scream, then they will kill me and maybe Ian if he comes running to my aid.

The interrogator stands up and nods to his cohorts that are holding my arms. One of them stands, while the other twists both arms painfully behind my back and drags me to my feet. The other rolls up his sleeves, and I notice the star tattoo on his wrist. Before I can say anything, he punches me hard in the face.

I stifle a scream, as blood explodes from my nose.

"What did you and the witch talk about?" The interrogator demands.

"Nothing! She was only here to bring me food!" I choke my head spinning.

"Wrong answer" He growls, while nodding to my assailant. Who cracks his knuckles before making a fist and punches me again.

Then things go incredibly blurry. I remember him asking me over and over what Mollie and I had talked about. Each time I didn't give the answers they want, they beat me harder and longer. I ride the wave of pain until I am thrown on the floor and my clothes are torn off. I feel another sharp pain in my head, and then; mercifully, I succumb to the darkness.

The next thing I remember is somewhere in the darkness Ian is calling my name, but it sounds like he is on the other end of a tunnel. I feel arms tenderly lift me up off the floor, as a shooting pain fills my body. I try to open my eyes, but they are swelled shut. I feel so weak and tired; I let the darkness take me again into its merciful depths.

Chapter 7

Ian

She drifts in and out of consciousness for days, while battling, not only her injuries, but also a raging fever. Whoever did this about beat her near to death. I found her curled up, naked, in a pool of blood, and her assailants were long gone. They are lucky they were. I feel so guilty and angry. I was only a few doors down, and did not hear this happening. I couldn't do anything to prevent it. I could not protect her. I am to blame for this.

"How is Jess?" Lucie asks, sitting up and rubbing her eyes.

We were staying in Jess' apartment while taking care of her, and protecting her from any more attacks. Lucie curls up beside Jess every night. She sings her a lullaby, like our nanny did when we were sick. I am so surprised she remembers it. She was young when they brought us here.

It has been such a great night. Before I left, I kissed Jess goodnight. I was hopeful for a new beginning for us together. Luce had been sleeping when I got home. I lay down next to her on the floor trying to sleep. I was so giddy and excited, that my heart was racing. I could still taste Jess' sweet kiss on my lips. If I couldn't sleep, why didn't I hear them attacking Jess? My mother always complained about the paper-thin walls here. There was an empty apartment between us…if I'd only heard…"

"Ian?" Lucie says, waking me from my reverie.

"What is it Luce?"

"Jess always ate the mushrooms from the cemetery. Do you think that's why this happened?" She asks, while her tiny pink lips quiver over the words.

"No, Luce." I answer calmly, scooting over so I can sit next to her and put my arms around her. "It's just the gangs. They do not know anything other than violence. "

"But, why did they do this to Jess? She is a good person. She didn't hurt anyone. She helps people!" Lucie's voice is full of indignation and sadness.

"I don't know Luce." I reply, drawing her closer to me. "I just don't know."

The next day Mollie comes by bringing a basket of carrots, a box of potatoes, and a small container of tiny strawberries that my sister loved so much. She became a daily visitor. She voices her anger repeatedly to me about what had happened to Jess. Mollie became quite fond of my little sister over the past week. Lucie is a gentle and kind soul; it is hard for anyone not to love her. She has always been this way. She was always popular with everyone when we were growing up, both adults and kids alike. When we were moved to the apartments, she easily made friends. I had a harder time. I was a loner, happier in my room with my sketchbook, than outside playing football and foursquare with everyone else. Then, I met Jess, and we became fast friends. She supported me when my parents died. When my older brother Andy died, she helped me bury him, not far from where we buried

Justilian. I kept Jess sane as she watched her entire family succumb to the wasting disease. We held each other, as they died one by one. First Mckenna died, and her brother Christopher soon after.

Her mother contracted the disease from working with dead bodies, and died a year after. Throughout that time, Jess remained stoic, only allowing herself to cry when she was alone with me. I would hold her as she sobbed into my chest cursing God, and the world that we lived in.

"Ian!" Luce demands.

"What is it kiddo?"

"Can I have some berries?"

"Eat just a few for now. We'll make them last, okay?" I answer, ruffling her hair and smiling at her.

She nods, and happily bounces off into the kitchen to pick some small ones to eat.

Mollie smiles at me. "She's pretty special, isn't she?"

"She sure is." I agree.

"Mollie, I want to ask you something."

"Sure, what is it?"

"I need to get antibiotics for Jess."

"Do you know what you're asking?" Mollie says, her voice fills with warning and trepidation

"Jess' life depends on it." I press. I know what the cost might be, and I am totally committed to getting them for her.

Getting the medicine meant we would need to go into the graveyard at night, and meet with Ash to get permission to enter the hospital. If he says yes, I know it means he will want something in return. I hope it isn't something dangerous, and takes me away from Jess.

Three days later, Mollie came to tell me she set up a meeting with Ash. The meeting would be taking place when the light faded over the cemetery the next evening. I knew it was important to get there before him to ensure the safety of the trade items I would be bringing. If I lost them, Jess would die.

He wants to meet at Justilian's grave, but I'm unsure of the reason why. Jess is getting worse every day, and I'm afraid we're going to lose her. I don't want to leave for the meeting, but I know I have to. This is a last ditch effort.

"Mollie, you're going to be staying here with Luce, right?" I ask her going over our list of things we needed to do.

"Absolutely darlin', dontcha worry bout' us I've got Angel watchin' over us."

"Angels aren't going to protect you if you get jumped in the apartment." I say in a concerned voice. "If that happens, I want you and Lucie to run. They'll leave Jess alone, because they won't want to mess with someone who's dying."

Molly laughs so hard I swear she is going to fall over. "Not angels. ANGEL, the Spanish lad who lives upstairs from you."

It was my turn to laugh this time. I knew Angel his biceps are as large as a tree trunk, and no one in the building will mess with him. I wonder how he knows Mollie. I'll bring it up later when I got back safely from the graveyard.

Chapter 8

Ian

I didn't realize how fast twenty-four hours could pass. While waiting for the meeting with Ash preparations keep me busy. There is so much I need to do before the meeting, such as locating some PDQ. I'd have to ask Mollie for her help with obtaining other supplies I can offer to Ash. I want to do everything I can to get on his good side. Getting the PDQ consists of making several strategic trades to get to my final goal. I end up with ten cans of spaghetti rings, some canned beans, two ten pound bags of sugar, two boxes of cookies, and a leather Jacket, which is packed carefully in Jess' cart. I tow it behind me as I walk through the empty graveyard to Justilian's grave.

The last time I came here, Justilian's body was carefully placed in this same cart. That time meant death, this one means life.

Even though the graveyard is deserted, I feel eyes watching me. I can't pinpoint their location, but I know I am surrounded.

Finally, I arrive at Justilian's grave, and I smile at the small white cross with blue flowers painted on it bearing Justilian's name. I know Jess took a great deal of time and attention while painting the details on his cross. There are hearts at the four corners. The words friend, brother, survivor, and forever were written inside the hearts. I brush away a tear thinking of Jess working on this beautiful marker, while trying to keep her tears from ruining the paint. She loved him like a brother in life; and now in death he became a saint.

The sound of footsteps invades my daydream. I turned to see Ash and four of his goons coming my way. Ash walks in the middle of the group with the four goons flanking him. Even at six feet one inch tall, Ash is small in comparison to his bodyguards.

I pull in a deep breath and try to put on a brave face. Inside, I am shaking like a leaf. As I was leaving for the meeting, Mollie warned me not to show my fear. Ash could smell fear a mile away.

"I heard you need a favor." Ash said, while leaning forward on a black cane with a silver dragon's head. His grey eyes glint-silver in the torchlight. He is very impressive in person.

"Yes." I reply, trying to sound brave. "I brought some supplies for trade."

Ash nods to an oversized redheaded goon on his left, who saunters over to Jess' wagon and rifles through the cache of supplies.

"Where'd ya get this?" The goon asks waving the case of PDQ in my face.

"Doesn't matter!" Ash booms "Leave him alone."

Usually, when caught with PDQ, the person is promptly beaten to a pulp. Therefore, I am shocked when Ash calls off his goon. I take a deep breath, and feel a little more of my courage return.

The goon carries the box of PDQ to Ash, who inspects the packages carefully, while making sure they are real. Real PDQ is getting harder to find. I was lucky to get any at all. It was probably stolen from Ash in the first place. He seems to have the monopoly on the PDQ market right now.

"So, this favor..." Ash says, putting the packages carefully back into the box. "What are you looking for?"

I count to ten, as I breathe in deeply, trying to still the terror that threatens to overtake me. How Mollie and Jess deal with Ash and his goons, I will never know.

"Rebel, I'm looking for safe passage into your territory." I say feigning confidence, and looking straight into his eyes.

"What for?" The red headed goon asks snarling at me, and taking a step forward.

Ash raises his hand.

"I need to get into the hospital. I need to find some antibiotics."

"You look pretty healthy to me!" The goon sneers.

Ash glares at the goon, and he shuts up immediately.

"Who are you getting them for?" Ash asks, with a hint of kindness in his voice.

"My friend Jess, she was beaten and raped, and she's barely hanging on. She's got some kind of infection, and a high fever." I tell him, trying to hide my rage. Every minute I waste, here is a minute I could be doing something productive to help Jess. I did not care how scared I am, Jess is going to die without antibiotics.

"Jess," Ash breathes as several emotions cross his face. I wonder what he is thinking. "You know who did it?"

"I wish I did, they'd be dead." I said, balling my hands into fists.

"They will be." I heard Ash mutter.

"The blind witch told me you were coming for medicine. I didn't know it was for Jess. How bad is it?" Ash asks.

"Bad enough," I state flatly. I was not willing to share the fact that Jess was dying with Ash and his goons.

Ash puts his hand in his coat pocket, and pulls out a large plastic zipper bag with a tall plastic bottle in it. He tosses it to me, and I catch it in midair.

"Jess saved my life once. She saved my little sister's life twice. If you need more, let one of my guys know." Ash says, staring straight into my eyes.

"Thank you," I stammer, astonished and unnerved at Ash's uncommon kindness.

"I'll send someone by each day to make sure you're safe, and see if you need anything. You still located in the fourth ward?"

I nod shocked at his complete change of demeanor.

"Good, and don't worry about getting revenge. You tell Jess I'll take care of it." Ash says, while punching his hand, "My sister and I are alive because of her. You're under our protection now."

Ash waves his hand at his goons signaling it is time to leave. As he begins walking away, his goons fall into step around him in what looks like a military maneuver.

"What about the supplies?" I yell, glancing down at the cartload of hard won items I brought.

"Keep em' you'll need em," Ash calls, not even bothering to turn around.

I stand there motionless, watching them disappear into the darkness, as feelings of shock and terror creep up on me. I grab Jess' cart, and run as fast as I can back to the apartment, eager to fill the others in on Ash's uncommon generosity.

The next few days pass very slowly. I am frustrated because there have been a few changes in Jess' condition. Her cuts and bruises are healing slowly, and her temperature has lowered a bit.

Ash keeps his promise. Every day his goons visit us, and I found out the name of the red headed goon is Charlie. Charlie brought us bandages, fresh water and food, and always inquired about Jess. He never would step inside the door, but he always speaks to me and brings a cart full of supplies. I think he is afraid of me, which is somewhat funny because he's twice my size.

Mollie stopped by frequently to visit us. It's nice to have her here to quell Lucie's innocent, worried chatter. She is so afraid that Jess is going to die. It wore on me with all that was going on, so to have the diversion was a blessing.

Lucie loves Mollie and vice versa. I wonder if Mollie had a brother or a sister once. She is very patient, and good to Lucie. She manages to find toys and books that keep Lucie entertained for hours. This gives us time to talk about the rumors that are spreading at the market about our alliance with Ash. She also tells me that there are gang members being beaten, or disappearing without a trace. Ash's work, I would guess.

About a week later, there is a loud pounding at the door. I motion to Lucie to hide in one of the back bedrooms.

"Open up Ian, damn it!" Ash's voice echoes through our entire apartment.

"I'm coming!" I yell going to the door after I see Lucie run down the hallway.

I open the door, and there stood Ash and two of his goons. Between the goons, there is a very battered looking member of the Demons.

"Tell him what you told me!" Ash orders.

The kid looks up at me with a mixture of fear and contempt. Blood drips from his nose, which is noticeably crooked.

"There's a death order for Jess and the Blind Witch." He growls.

"Why? What for?" I ask shaken, as a chill runs down my spine.

"Because, they sell PDQ with that guy Justilian." The boy spat back, "I seen 'em myself!"

"No, they weren't!" I yell, losing it on the kid, while getting in his face. ""If you forgot, I was there, too! Justilian used it to feed hungry and sick kids. That's mainly when he actually had the stuff."

"Easy kid," Ash says, grabbing my fist firmly. I had unconsciously raised it to pummel the kid.

I take a step back, seething as Ash steps between the battered Demon and I.

"Kid...you have your facts wrong. If one of you Demons dares to lay a hand on either the witch or the girl, you will lose. Don't even think about touching anyone in this apartment or there will be war!" Ash says in a threatening tone. "Now, if you would kindly get off my turf before I give the boys the okay to rip off your arms, it would be much appreciated."

The goons drop the kid unceremoniously on the ground. He glares at me, and takes off running. Ash snaps to his goons who stand on either side of the door as he walks into the apartment closing the door behind him. The goons remain stationed outside.

"How is Jess?" He asks.

"Not much change, her fever's down."

"You usin' the medicine?"

"Yes, I mix it with water, and feed it to her with a spoon."

"Try doubling it." Ash suggests, "Can I see her?"

"Sure," I answer, leading him to the living room where Jess lays on her makeshift bed.

Ash kneels beside her and takes her hand gently in his. He looks at her with a tenderness that surprises me.

"I'm sorry kid." He whispers. "This shouldn't have happened."

"Ash, how do you know Jess?" I ask.

"Before all this…" he says haltingly. " She and I went to school together."

"You did?" I ask.

"Yeah, she was pretty much a loner. She treated me good." Ash answers.

"She's like that." I agree.

"She's special." He whispers, "one of a kind."

"You love her, don't you?" I ask.

"How could anyone not?" He says, "She's beautiful inside and out. Even after everyone died, she would scavenge food, and share it with others. She never hoarded or stole that I know of. She never let the state of the world get to her. She never fell prey to any of it. She stayed…good." He finishes.

"Yes, she has always been that way." I agree.

"Do you think she'll make it?" Ash asks.

"I don't know. She's been sleeping for so long."

A loud crash in one of the bedrooms brings us to our feet.

"Come out!" Ash yells, drawing a large hunting knife from a hidden sheath near his knee.

"Easy Ash…" I warn, putting my hand on his arm. "It's just my sister Lucie."

Timidly, Lucie came out of the bedroom, her eyes fearful and full of tears.

"Luce, what happened?" I ask keeping a firm grip on Ash's arm that holds the knife. I was amazed his goons didn't rush in too.

"There were some shelves. I backed into them, and they fell down." Luce says nervously.

"Are you okay?" I ask, letting go of Ash's arm and stepping forward, putting myself between Ash and my little sister.

"Yes." She whispers quickly. Then runs down the hallway towards us, and hides in my arms, while staring at Ash through wide, frightened eyes.

"It's okay kiddo…" Ash says, kneeling down in front of her. "I won't hurt you."

He reaches into his pocket, and pulls out another large plastic bag.

"Here you take this." He says, "I bet you forgot all about candy."

Lucie looks at Ash, and then looks at me. I nod. Tentatively, she steps forward toward Ash, and timidly takes the bag from him.

"Thank you." She says her voice barely above a whisper.

"I had a little sister, too. She liked candy a lot just like you." Ash offers.

"What happened to her?" I ask, maneuvering Lucie behind me.

"She died of pneumonia after my mother died. Now, it's only Angie and I." Ash said, his voice seeming far away. "You enjoy that sweetie and you let me know when you run out." He says, smiling at Lucie "I'll get you more."

"Thank you," I say, putting my arm around Lucie, who is staring at the bag of candy with wide eyes.

"No problem." Ash said standing up, at six feet one inch he is quite an imposing figure.

"You need anything, you let me know." He says gruffly.

"I will. Thank you for everything." I answer slowly.

Before either of us can say anything, Lucie bolts from my side, and hugs a very surprised Ash. He reaches down tenderly, and returns Lucie's gentle gesture.

I see a tear slip down Ash's cheek. He is not as heartless as everyone thinks he is.

A few days later, I am lying beside Jess while holding her hand, as I always did. The candlelight lit her face with an ethereal glow, making her look like a porcelain doll. She looks so peaceful lying there. I wonder if she was dreaming, and what she might be dreaming of.

I feel a slight squeeze on my hand. Initially, I jump, because I was not expecting it, then I look over at Jess who begins stirring.

"Jess?" I whisper, sitting up slowly, and moving into her field of vision, so she does not panic.

Her eyes flutter open. She looks confused and blinks several times, before turning her head slightly to focus her gaze on me.

"Hey Jess." I whisper, as relief washes over me. I brush a stray hair out of her face.

"Ian?" She whispers hoarsely, lifting her hand to her throat and wincing in pain.

"How are you feeling?" I ask anxiously.

"Thirsty." She whispers, her eyes still trying to focus on me.

I pick up my canteen, and give her a small sip of water. She drinks it gratefully. Then, she coughs while crying out slightly from the pain in her throat. I tried getting enough water in her while she was unconscious, but I was doing it with a spoon.

"How long?" She rasps, while holding her throat.

"Three weeks." I answer, offering her some more water. "Do you remember what happened?"

"Yes." She whispers, as a tear slides down her cheek.

"It's all right." I said, as I gently brushed away her tears. "You're safe now. I'll never leave you unprotected again!"

"You can't promise that." She whispers bitterly. "No one can promise that."

"I sure can. I've got the power of Rebel on my side." I say in mock confidence. "We're under his protection."

"Ash, really?" Jess asks surprised.

"Yeah, who knew beneath that cool marble exterior, Ash would have a marshmallow heart." I said, smiling at her as she closes her eyes wearily and falls into a light slumber.

"Rest well, Jess." I murmur, kissing her forehead before laying back down beside her.

The next morning, I send word through one of Rebel's henchmen that Jess woke up. I'm not sure what the response will be, I hope he isn't going to come over and drill Jess for descriptions of her attackers. She needs rest in order to heal both her mind and her body. I hope Ash's visit will not hinder her recovery. I was not even sure if she remembers anything about her attackers.

Chapter 9

Jess

The week after I woke up everything seemed to be a blur. There are numerous visits from Molly, because of the supplies coming and going. Ian constantly flitted around the apartment, fussing over me like an old biddy hen. The nightmares are always waiting to haunt me every time I close my eyes.

Ian holds me in the candlelight when I wake up screaming and crying, while covered in sweat. He spends the nights stroking my hair, and whispering quiet words of reassurance in my ear.

Nothing seemed to work to erase the terror of that night. It is burned into my memory, and I don't understand why I was chosen for their wrath. I can't remember anything after them rushing into my house. My mind remembers pieces, like it's protecting itself. The memories only resurface in my dreams, because my mind lets its guard down. The puzzle pieces can fit together in a cohesive pattern when it happens.

"Jess," Lucie says, waking me from my reverie. She extends a cup of hot vegetable broth to me.

I take it and smile at her gratefully. Through all of this, Lucie is the one I worry about the most. She's changed so much. She seems more fearful and timid than ever. I vow to myself to protect her, even if it means giving up my own life. Her innocence can never be stolen the way mine was. No one will ever be allowed to hurt her.

"Jess, are you going to die?" She asks me tearfully, while her lips quiver.

I suck in a deep breath, and look at her, while wiping the tears from her cheeks. "No Lucie, I'm not going to die. I'm going to be just fine. I'm getting better every day."

"My mom said she was getting better too, but then…" She chokes back a sob.

I grab her and pull her to me. As I hold her trembling body to my shoulder, I rub her back as she sobs. She has lost her mother, father, older brother, and her entire world. Her innocence was unfairly taken from her. Her perfect world was shattered by the virus.

There is nothing I can do to change that, but in this moment, if I can fill the void and be what she needs; then I will.

Chapter 10

Ian

I see Lucie and Jess curled up together, sound asleep when I come home late that afternoon from my meeting with Mollie at the Trader's Den. She shared some interesting information that more survivors were getting addicted to some new form of P.D.Q. which was made by a rising new gang called the Zombies. It's called Necromancer, and it's hitting the streets fast.

Ash warned me in the past to be wary of the Zombies, because they never ask you to join. They force you to join. If you aren't in a gang, you are targeted to be "culled" as a Zombie. The word on the street is that many people don't survive the initiation.

I put down the bag of carrots and potatoes Mollie gave me, along with the box of strawberries she sent back for Lucie on the counter in the kitchen. Before I got to Jess', I stopped at my old apartment, and put the other various items Mollie gave us in my old bedroom. My old home made an awesome storage unit, as long as no one found out it is unoccupied and full of supplies. I try to make it seem like I am coming and going from there frequently, so no one suspects what it is really used for.

Jess has been regaining her strength very quickly, which is a good thing, because I want to include her in my plan. Right now, stressing her out will make it harder for her. Ash, Mollie, and I have been working on this project for a while now, and I hope Jess will be on board with the scheme that is going to unravel quickly in the near future.

I start peeling the carrots and potatoes to make soup, and then I chop up some of the onions and tomatoes that Ash brought to us yesterday. I think how funny it is for me to be cooking now. When my parents were alive, we had a cook who made all of our meals for us. You cannot have the wife of a diplomat cooking her own meals now could you? My dad had reluctantly taken the appointment, but he was happier working with the different causes and charities that he and my mother had adopted long ago when his law firm was profitable. We lived in a big house out in the suburbs, and he would commute to the city, usually staying there for several days. I suspected this is where he picked up the virus. He came home one weekend looking very tired and pale, and he passed away within a month. When the consulate found out he had contracted the virus, everyone treated us like pariahs. They moved all of us in the dead of night to the tenements. My mother was pregnant, and we hoped the baby would give her some immunity; but she too got the virus and died in childbirth leaving my brother Andy, Lucie, and I alone. The virus took Andy shortly after my mother died, I think because he was the one who looked after her, and he would not let Lucie and I into our mother's room. Lucie was too young to remember the nannies, the cooks, and our life before all of this; and I am glad. I look over at her contentedly sleeping next to Jess, and smile. I'm glad we are going to be a family. I have wanted this for a long time. I have been too afraid to say anything; and now that I did, I am afraid I am going to lose everything like I did before.

There's a loud knocking at the door. Lucie wakes with a start and instinctively runs down the hall to the back bedroom. We taught her to do this right after the goons went after Jess. We want her to be safe, and if something happens to us, we hope they won't think of looking back there behind the piles of furniture. I rush over to Jess and quickly help her to her feet before looking out the security pinhole in the door. I breathe a sigh of relief when I see one of Ash's bodyguards at the door. Ash calls him Bullitt, I think and that's because he has a shaved head, but one could never be too sure about where any of the gang members got their names. Bullitt is one the largest bodyguards Ash has. He has become a frequent visitor to the apartment, always bringing us something from Ash. However, I believe it has something to do with Mollie. Today is no different. He puts down two heavy sacks of supplies on the floor in the foyer.

"Do you want to stay and eat?" Jess asks limping into the kitchen. "We have some vegetable soup."

"Nah," he said, "I gotta get back, there's a war council brewing."

"War council," I asked. "What for?"

"Yeah, those damn Zombies are cuttin' into everyone's territory, s'time to cut them down."

"Who's going to the council?" Jess asks looking at me anxiously.

"Us, The Skulls, Flames, Rebels, and some smaller gangs who want to align with us." Bullitt answers.

"How bad is it?" I asked, trying to remain aloof.

"Bad enough, they're killin' our workforce and takin' our stuff." Bullitt answers bitterly. "They ain't gonna be stealin' nuthin' from us. This is our territory."

I look at Jess. I can see the wheels turning in her head, and that is never good. She bit her tongue and I'm glad, because she never believed in the slave labor that the gangs used to gain a foothold through P.D.Q. distribution. Jess is very vocal, and outspoken about her feelings on that subject. I'm always afraid that it will get her in trouble.

"I better get back; Ash'll be lookin' for me." Bullitt said. "You need anything else?"

"No we're okay." I answer, offering him my hand.

He looks at me, and takes it awkwardly.

"Let me know if ya do, and by the way, I'd double lock this door tonight. It's not gonna be safe on the streets for anyone tonight."

His words send chills down my spine. There is a war coming. I can feel it. I will make sure to double lock the door behind him.

Chapter 11

Jess

We eat our dinner in silence. I catch Ian stealing glances at me over his soup while we dip pieces of French bread, which Ash sent with Bullitt, into the thin broth. I know that bread is a very expensive commodity, and I wonder where he got it. There's a great deal of tension in the air, and we are both very anxious after our conversation with Bullitt. Even Lucie feels the chill in the air. I see her stealing glances at Ian and I with fear in her eyes. The war council meant bad things were coming. I am afraid, not only for myself, but for everyone in the city. I'm worried that there will be no way that I can keep doing Justilian's work, when the gangs were in an uproar. Ian double-checks the locks before we put Lucie to bed.

"What do you think is going to happen?" Ian asks.

"I don't know but it can't be anything good."

"I think a war is coming…" Ian begins his voice filled with fear, which was so unlike Ian.

"And the survivors in this city are going to be the casualties." I finish for him.

"Yeah."

"You've been going to the market a lot." I said, trying to change the subject, and maybe lighten the mood.

"We needed supplies." Ian explains simply.

"I think we have more than enough."

"Not if we're going to leave the city."

"What are you talking about?" I asked, knowing there is no way we can leave. I made a promise to Justilian.

"Mollie and I have been talking. We need to leave the city." Ian says.

"Is it that bad?" I asked. "Isn't there anything we can do?"

"Worse than bad, it's going to make World War II look like a party. The Zombies are stronger than they are letting on. They have cells outside the city, and we think they are only making a weak showing in the city to fool the gangs that are in control here. They're going to take over, and it's not going to be pretty."

"Where would we go?" I ask. Suddenly, a lump forms in my throat, as my heartbreaks knowing my promise couldn't be kept.

"Mollie and I've been talking about The Promised Land."

"But, we don't even know where it is?"

"Mollie knows how to get there. She said if we leave the city and go northwest, we'll find our way."

"Mollie?"

"She's had her ear to the ground for us. She's coming with us." Ian said.

"Really?" I ask. Mollie is the last person I thought would think of leaving the city.

"Yeah, I was waiting for the right time to tell you so I didn't upset you. I'm sorry I waited for so long." Ian said apologetically.

"You should have told me." I said angrily.

"Are you angry with me?"

"A little, I mean I could have helped you get the supplies."

"And put an even bigger target on your back." Ian finishes. "Besides you're not even healed yet, and you can't move through the city like I can!"

Ian is right; whatever I am wanted for, I know that if they see me at the market still alive and kicking; I will have a target on my back. I shudder at the thought of going through that again and maybe not surviving this time. My biggest fear is Lucie or Ian being killed on my account.

"A penny for your thoughts?" Ian ask, gently touching my face, and bringing me back to reality.

"Nothing, I'm not going to admit that you're right!" I tease, punching him in the arm.

"You never do." He says, catching my hand and pulling me close to him.

"When are we leaving?" I asked, laying my head on his chest, and listening to the steady thrum of his heart.

"In the next day or two, with the war council, we need to get out before the fighting starts." He answers.

"Yeah" I agree, "It won't be safe for us to travel by day. Maybe Ash will give us safe passage through the graveyard to get out of the city."

"I'll talk to him tomorrow." Ian said "I hope he'll be at the Trader's Den, if not we'll have to go it on our own."

A chill passes down my spine; the graveyards at night are a dangerous place. There are so many gangs in there that could jump you, and leave you for dead, and no one would ever know. It is taboo to travel through them, unless you are burying your own dead. Not to mention how huge of an area we will have to cover. No one knows how big the graveyards are. No one travels to the end, and has come back to tell the story. Most are thought to be lost, or taken by evil spirits that are said to linger there to protect the dead. Instinctively, I pull away from him.

"Jess, don't think about it right now. Just rest, you need to get stronger for the trip." Ian said, breaking into my thoughts.

"Yeah… right." I thought. "The only sleep I'll get tonight is going to be filled with nightmares."

He pulls me even closer and I lay my head on his chest while listening again to his heart. The sound is so soothing, and his warmth surrounds me like a blanket, making me feel safe. Thankfully, I drift off into a dreamless slumber.

Chapter 12

Jess

A huge commotion in the hallway wakes us early the next morning. Ian rushes to the door and looks out the peephole. Lucie is nearly in my lap. Her whole body is trembling.

"There are people scrambling everywhere." Ian said anxiously. "I hear people running."

A loud pounding on the door interrupts him. He jumps back.

Ian looks at me for help, and I motion for him to look through the peephole. When he is nervous, his brain always blanks out.

Seconds later, Bullitt, and a swearing, panting, disheveled Mollie are standing in my kitchen.

I scramble to my feet. "What happened?"

I limp into the kitchen and steady Mollie, who looks as if she is going to fall down. She pushes me away mumbling and cursing, as she tries fruitlessly to rearrange her skirt and fix her hair that has fallen in knots over her face.

"What happened is this lunkhead here yanked me outta my bed at this ungodly hour!" Mollie shrieks gesticulating wildly. "Then he dragged me clear across town like a sack of potatoes!"

"Oh shut UP you Irish banshee. I'm surprised the whole city didn't hear you!" Bullitt said, shaking his head in frustration. "If I hadn't saved your ass you'd be dead by now!"

"What do you mean?" Ian asked I could hear him breathing very quickly.

"The Zombies were gunning for her and the lot of you as well!" Bullitt said angrily

"Why?" I asked, shocked that yet another gang is after me. What had I done that is so horrible? I helped people. I saved lives. I want to make Justilian proud of me, but at what cost?

"You go against everything they stand for, and you're causing quite a riot. People are rebelling. They won't work for us no more!" Bullitt explains angrily. "They are taking what they want now!"

Ian and I smile conspiratorially at the unguarded truth of his words.

"What about the war council?" I ask, trying to redirect Bullitt's anger.

"The Zombies raided it. There's a lotta gang chiefs dead, and even more on the run. Rebel himself was run outta the city."

"He was run out of town?" I ask. Ash never backed down to anyone.

"It won't last long. He's runnin the whole outfit from the grave lands." Bullitt said defiantly. "We were lucky we had a hideout out there. It's not comfortable, but it's home for now. We gotta be slick comin in and out of the city, but slick ain't hard when it comes to Rebel."

"Now Banshee." Bullitt says, turning to Mollie who is mumbling and cursing under her breath. "Will ya quit your caterwauling and stay put till it's safe for ya go back to whatever you were doing?"

Mollie glares at Bullitt, and then sits down hard on the kitchen chair I offer her. I'm amazed it doesn't break!

"What about me shop?" She asks venomously.

"Don't worry; we'll have someone run it for ya." Bullitt says exasperated.

"Ya don't know a fair trade to save your immortal souls!" Mollie says angrily, wielding her stick like a broadsword. I duck to get out of the way. It ends up touching the tip of Bullitt's nose. I don't know how she accomplishes this, but she has great aim for a blind girl.

"Yeesh!" Bullitt curses, throwing his arms up in frustration. "How're ya gonna run it from here?"

"You cheat my customers; I'll make sure you burn in hell." She threatens.

"Whatever, Banshee!" He breathes.

I can see that he is trying to decide whether to take Mollie down or not. I knew he wouldn't, it will be bad for his rep.

"What'd you say?" She counters angrily, never removing her stick from his nose.

"Yes, I'll take care of it myself." He answers patronizingly.

"Ya better." She warns lowering her stick slowly.

"I've gotta go. Make sure the Banshee stays put, will ya? I don't want to be on Rebel's bad side, because something happened to her."

I nod.

"Ya need anything, ya know where to ask." He says before closing the door behind him.

Chapter 13

Ian

Taking care of Mollie is easy calming her down is not. I do not understand how Jess tolerates her. During the first few hours she is with us, she is constantly fussing over the state of affairs at her store. How Bullitt would not make a fair trade, and then she would lose her all her customers. Finally, Jess got her to set her mind on keeping all the supplies we had gathered in some sort of "Godly order." Her family must have been religious, because she keeps using the almighty's name in vain every chance she got. But, then again, she is Irish.

"Mollie, do you want to get set up in the living room with us, or do you want to stay in a different area?" I ask hoping that maybe a good night's sleep will calm the angry she devil that lives in Mollie.

"Why don't I stay in that other storehouse you have?" Mollie says hopefully. "And we don't want anyone getting wind of what's over there.

"Mollie, you know Ash wants you stay in this apartment." Jess pipes up as she goes about trying to make more room in the living room where we all sleep. This is a huge, daunting task considering what a small space it is.

"Would you mind settin me up in one of the bedrooms? I snore." She answers, quietly trying to control her anger.

"That's fine Mollie, Jess, and I will move stuff around while you and Lucie make lunch. How does that sound?" I suggest.

"Sounds like a fine idea, come on sweet pea lets cook us some fancy faire for our feast." Mollie says, smiling at me.

"I'll teach ya how to cook a fine Irish meal."

Lucie followed her to the kitchen, laughing and chattering behind her.

As we walk down the hallway, Jess giggled, "You know you snore, too."

"Would you like to sleep somewhere else, maybe bunk with Mollie?" I offer, teasingly.

"Nah, your snoring makes the quiet more beautiful." Jess says, punching my arm.

I grab her and spin her around until I have her pinned up against the wall. "So, you like my snoring do ya?"

"Yeah I do." She says, blushing trying to avoid eye contact with me.

I steal a quick kiss, and run down the hall to the back bedroom. She giggles and runs after me. I catch her again, kissing her more deeply this time.

"You know I love you." I murmur.

Jess smiles up at me shyly. Gently, she takes my face in her hands, and kisses me again. It is so innocent and hopeful; I draw in a sharp breath.

Jess steps backwards, frightened. I catch her arm. We stand there staring into each other's eyes lost in the moment.

Loud cursing from Mollie in the kitchen brings us back to reality.

"We better get moving." Jess stammers.

I back up trying to control my breathing that somehow become very shallow and rapid.

"Yeah," I agree, putting my head down on hers.

We manage to move most of the shelving into the smaller bedroom, so Mollie will have plenty of room to navigate around her room safely, without tripping over anything. We took the old bed frame, and lay one of the heavier shelves into it creating a makeshift pallet bed for Mollie, so she will not be on the floor. If she is going to stay with us, she should at least be comfortable.

While Jess is finishing the bedroom, I venture to my other apartment, which is well stocked. I scrounge a few new sleeping bags, and a pillow for Mollie to use. I do not know how many of her things will be obtainable from her apartment, or how much Bullitt would be bringing for her.

As I was coming out of the apartment, I freeze. I see two big guys with white faces, dressed all in black leather, coming out of the stairwell. I step back into my apartment and wait while staring out the peephole to see where they are going. They stop for a moment by Jess' apartment, but quickly move on down the hall to the next stairwell. I wait for what seems like an eternity to make sure they are gone. Then, quickly book it back to Jess'.

I run into the back bedroom, dodging around Mollie and Lucie in the kitchen. I put down the sleeping bags, then go over to the door and shut it as quietly as I can, before turning to face a very confused looking Jess.

"Jess, I think the Zombies are patrolling the building." I whisper.

"Why?" She asks, her eyes widening.

"I saw two HUGE guys with extremely scary white faces coming down the hall when I was coming back, and they didn't look too friendly."

"So, what does that mean for us?"

"I really don't know, but we've got to get out of here. They stopped in front of here, but then kept going. I don't know if they're planning something, or if they are watching us." I said quietly. I didn't want Lucie to hear and get scared, the last thing I need was for Lucie to freak out.

"We've got to find a way to move and pack quickly without anyone seeing." Jess says sounding worried.

"And I have the perfect idea for that." I answer, pulling out the saw I grabbed when I went back into my apartment.

"Are you nuts? What are we going to do, build a catwalk?" Jess asks in disbelief.

"Not exactly" I answer, pointing to the back wall of the bedroom. "This backs up to the empty apartment next door, all we have to do is make a hole in the wall, and then make another hole in the other side. Then we've got a concealed walkway to bring all the supplies over here." I explain.

"And this won't make a ton of noise, and be very conspicuous?" Jess answers sarcastically, looking at the saw doubtfully.

"We're on the outside corner. We will be fine. We'll do it today right after lunch when everyone is moving around, no one will hear us." I said.

"I don't know what we're going to find in that other apartment." Jess said. "For all we know there are rotting bodies in there."

"I guess we'll find out when we make our first hole." I answer simply.

"All right," Jess says slowly, not agreeing I'm right. She knew the imminent danger we are in and seems willing to take this obvious risk.

"We need to do this fast Jess, and get out of here. This way none of us gets killed. I have a terrible feeling that something is going to happen, and it's going to happen soon."

Chapter 14

Jess

It takes almost two days to break through the apartment wall. Every time Ian grumbles, I remind him it *was his* idea. When we break through to the other apartment, we find it had been ransacked, but all the important items had been stowed in between the walls, which makes it harder to get through. These are some resourceful survivors! We end up coming out with more than enough to cover the four of us for the journey west. The parents of these kids must have been in the medical field, because we find a veritable storehouse of all kinds of medicines, bandages, peroxide, alcohol, and a number of other first aid items in the walls. The apartment smells of mothballs, which is what they used to deter the mice from eating their stuff. I am glad we do not find any dead bodies in the apartment, because that would have definitely been a deal breaker right there.

Mollie keeps Lucie busy all day, so she will be out of our way while we are moving the supplies into the smaller back bedroom. I bring my cart into the apartment, piece by piece at different times of the day, so people will not notice what I am doing. I especially did not want the Zombies getting wind of what we are doing. I am terrified of what they will do to us if they knew how much we have. Maybe, they will come and raid us, kill us, and make it look like another gang did it.

"Jess, hurry up! There's someone at the door!" Ian urges as I come through the wall with a load of canned goods in my arms.

I quickly brush myself off before I walk out into the kitchen area where Ian and Mollie are entertaining a tall boy with white blonde hair, and striking fluorescent blue eyes. I stop dead in my tracks. I know those eyes.

"Where ya been?" The boy asks trying to sound tough.

"Bathroom" I answer thinking quickly. "And believe me you *DON'T* want to go back there anytime soon!"

"This is Bullitt's brother Dagger. He came to see if we needed anything." Ian says introducing the boy who strikes terror into my soul.

I take a moment to think, trying to drive the memory from my head. "We could surely use more candles and some more candy for Lucie."

"I thought ya might say that," Dagger growls, pulling out a shopping bag of candy. "The boss sent this along."

Lucie jumps up and down giddily, and runs into the living room. She reappears with a card for Ash. "Make sure you give this to him." She directs, looking at Dagger wistfully.

Lucie worked for hours on this card. She is very fond of Ash. I smile at her through the anxiety and fear that is working its way through my outer shell. I know those eyes. I remember them. I want to snatch her away from him.

Ian can feel my body tense up, and looks at me anxiously.

"What's wrong with her?" Dagger asks.

"Long day, she's afraid of the Zombies taking over." Ian explains. "She's been sick with worry over it."

"Where's the other lug?" Mollie asks brusquely.

"He hadda go do a job for Rebel. He'll be around tomorrow." Dagger answers. "You should be afraid of them Zombies. I hear they skin little girls alive."

Lucie shrieks and hides behind Mollie's skirts. Mollie puts an arm around her protectively, and glares at Dagger.

I step forward between Dagger and Mollie. "You better not mess with Lucie, Ash is very fond of her, and if he heard you were scaring her for no reason, I don't think he would be very happy about it."

Dagger backs off mumbling a halfhearted apology.

"You better get going before I take a stick to ya!" Mollie yells angrily. "No one messes with my Lucie."

Mollie raises her walking stick and threatens Dagger, who drops the knapsack of supplies on the floor and backs out the door quickly. Ian slams the door behind him.

I breathe a sigh of relief after Dagger left. I know his eyes! I know who he is. He hovered over me while I was pinned to the floor helpless, hitting me repeatedly, interrogating me about Mollie and I had planned. I fell sobbing to my knees.

Ian's strong arms encircle me. "What's wrong?" He whispers frantically.

"He...he was one of them." I sob.

"One of who child?" Mollie asks, putting her hand on my shoulder in an effort to soothe me.

"The boys who came here" I choke out. "The ones who….who…"

"Oh…my…God..." Ian breathes, as his arms turn to steel around me.

"Ian don't, don't leave." I plead. "Please, I need you here."

Ian's arms slacken the tiniest bit. "I will kill him." He murmurs angrily.

"No, Ian please, we're leaving we're going far away from here. You need to survive, for me."

All of the sudden, a wave of nausea passes over me. I jump up jerking myself out of Ian's arms. I ran to the bathroom, and soon everything I had eaten all day is staring back at me. Ian comes in behind me. I can hear the water running in the sink.

"Jess," he says, pulling me into his arms while flushing the toilet. He holds a cup of water to my lips.

I sip it gratefully.

"Come on, we'll get you set up in the other bedroom. You can be near the bathroom." He says, calmly helping me to my feet.

I fall to my knees again, throwing up the little bit of water I just took in.

"It's okay, Jess," he soothes guiding me to my feet. "He will never hurt you again."

Ian helps me to lay down on Mollie's pallet. I feel guilty taking her rightful place; after all, we made it for her. He puts a cool cloth on my head, and then lies down beside me. He starts rubbing my back and shoulders, like my mother did when I was sick.

"It's all right Jess, just rest now." He soothes.

I lay my head on his shoulder. I am so exhausted. I've been so tired lately. Wearily, I close my eyes and let sleep take me.

Chapter 15

Jess

I awaken to Mollie gently replacing the washcloth on my forehead. She was crooning the most beautiful lullaby to Lucie. Mollie has not slept in this room since she came here. She wants to be near Lucie. She became a mother figure to Lucie, and they adore one another. I look up at the window and see it is night.

"Where's Ian?" I cough.

My throat feels like I swallowed razor blades, and my stomach feels as if it turned inside out. Every inch of my body aches and I am covered in a cold sweat. I hope this will not hold up our traveling. We need to get out of the city and fast!

"He's finishin' the packin'. We're leavin' tonight." Mollie answers gently putting her hand on my shoulder.

I try to get up, but I am hit by an instant wave of dizziness. My head begins throbbing, and the room is beginning to spin. Darkness is threatening to overtake me.

"Easy." Ian says, appearing from nowhere and catching me in his arms. "You're still weak."

"Ian." I whisper.

"Shhh, Jess you're in shock. It's been a rough day; one of a lot more to come." Ian murmurs, kissing me gently on the cheek and bringing a glass of water to my lips. "Everything is going to be all right."

The coolness of his touch is so soothing. I feel a little better. Ian helps me to sit up, having me lean against him for support.

"When are we going?" I ask weakly. I'm really not sure I want to do this. I do not think we will be successful doing this, and I am pretty sure what we are going to do is going to get us killed.

"Just before dawn, hopefully the gangs will be out of the cemetery, so we can get through there safely." Ian answers.

"And if not?" I ask panic filling my voice.

"Then, we'll hide where we can." Mollie answers. "Those graveyards are full of hidin' spots, and I know many of em'."

"What about Lucie?" I ask. "Will she be able to make the trip with us?"

"She's protected." Mollie says reassuringly. "She knows this is what we need to do. She's stronger than you think she is."

I nod my consent. I always thought of Lucie as my baby sister. Little girls grow up, unfortunately, now more quickly than ever. We need to be extra careful with her, because we don't want to get caught. I don't want to see her sold into the sex trade that is very predominant in the city.

"Then, let's do this." I say quickly before I change my mind. If we get caught, I will fight to my death to keep Lucie safe and shed my blood to make sure Ian will be safe, too.

We let Lucie sleep as we pack everything in the two carts we will be taking with us. Somehow, Mollie was able to procure a very large cart, even though she has been trapped inside our apartment. She can be very persuasive with Bullitt when she wants to. Ian and I broke into fits of giggles when Mollie told Bullitt she needed it so she can see what he is trading and monitor all the larger transactions. "To keep you honest," she said. "You're not to be trusted."

Mollie has been our rock this whole time, keeping us calm and teaching us the tricks of her trade. Ian has become very good at trading to get what we need and in the amounts that will sustain us while we traveled to the 'promised land', wherever that is. I know this is the right decision, but I don't know if this is the way we are supposed to do it. Maybe we should have thought about that sooner, gotten Ash's approval, and maybe a bunch of goons to protect us from whatever is out there. There are so many unknowns. I don't do well with the unknown. I would rather have a map, a plan, and maybe even an itinerary! Yeah right, no one knows exactly how big the cemetery is and there is no map. We don't have explorers like Columbus and Neil Armstrong. I laugh bitterly at the thought as I get up and make my way to my old bedroom. The one occupied by Mollie, I go to the far corner and pull up the floorboard. Inside is a small tin box. It holds my father's watch, pictures of my family, my mother's Bible, and pictures of my brother and sister.

These are all little reminders of the life I used to have. I wonder if Ian had something like this, something to carry him through when he thought all hope was lost. My mother read her Bible every day after my father died. She was a true woman of faith. I am very different, a lot like my father. He needed proof to back up the faith. He would always say, "Faith without proof is pointless." I did not believe that, heck I was not sure what to believe anymore.

Chapter 16

Ian

Jess has been battling terrifying nightmares since Dagger's visit. I know her brain is protecting itself, but need to connect the dots in the holes in her memory. Unfortunately, that means never ending nightmares. When she wakes up screaming, all I can do is cradle her in my arms and sooth-her pain as best I can. It was killing me inside to see her suffering. She hasn't been eating very well, and what she does eat comes right back up. She is exhausted all the time, and her body aches sometimes to the point of tears for her. I'm very worried about her. I hope this is not the beginning of the wasting sickness. If it is, I won't let her die in this rotting hellhole of a city. She deserves better than that. -

I put down what seems like the hundredth bag of potatoes into Mollie's cart.

"How many of these do you have?" I ask her.

"Enough." She answers, smiling at me. I swear I can see her milky eyes glitter. "Should I wake the wee one?"

I nod halfheartedly. "Yes, I think it's time."

I look over at Jess who's tying a thick burlap tarp over her small cartload of necessities. She hid her box filled with important things that she can't bear to leave behind in her cart. Even though it's small, it brings her hope. She looks up and smiles at me. Her confidence is somewhat reassuring, but I still have questions about this being the right move. If we all get killed, it will be because I didn't plan this well enough.

Lucie's arms around my waist wakes me from my reverie. I can feel her warmth, and her love through that one simple gesture.

"All right, Lucie goose. Let's get you in the cart. Remember, you need to be really quiet." I whisper, reminding her even though she's half-asleep. She nods slowly, then walks over and rolls up her bedroll in a cute zombie like fashion. After that, she picks up her bear and bag of candy that has gotten quite large, and comes back. I help her up into the wagon and she curls up in the niche I built for her. A small shelf rolls over the top her to conceal her in case of trouble. We have practiced using it until she became very good at concealing herself in a hurry. We make sure she can't be seen close up or at a distance. It is quite a little bit of genius, if I did say so myself. Necessity is the mother of invention.

    With Lucie safely secreted away and sound asleep, we are ready to go. Jess and Mollie will leave first with their small wagon. Then, I am scheduled leave fifteen minutes later, because I will be closer to the meeting point, which is Justilian's grave. Jess will come in from the other end of the city and meet me there. Then, we will travel together the rest of the way.

Chapter 17

Jess

"Meet at Justilian's grave" plays through my head. "Take the west entrance into the cemetery."

This place has an entrance? If it does, I've never seen it. The graves literally surround the city and every street ends at a different section of graveyard. There is no way to avoid walking through it or even around it, and no one knows how far out or how large the cemetery is The city's life is completely surrounded by death. Maybe, it is the sign of the human condition itself. I look at Mollie; she's so brave in spite of it all. We haven't seen any frightening white-faced members of the Zombies, and that is good, but not very reassuring. The rumors are that they have control of this part of the city. In fact, there aren't any gang members at all. The lack of any life in the streets at all sends a chill down my spine.

"It's too quiet." I whisper to Mollie. "Something doesn't feel right."

"We'd best be goin'." She whispers back. "We need to meet Ian and get out of here before we're all dug under."

Mollie pulls me in the direction she wants to go, her steps cautious, but confident. She knows this end of the tenements, and that gives me a little reassurance. She said this part of the tenements is on her trading route, and is a relatively safe route. I have no idea where we are going. I have never been here before, and now it is a classic case literally of the blind leading the blind. I couldn't help but to laugh at the irony of it.

"Are you sure this is safe?" I asked Mollie for about the hundredth time, as we walk down to the end of the street and into a row of ornately decorated mausoleums. These are the graves of the rich people, those that could be buried in style. These people were able to pay the death dealers to make sure they had a proper burial.

"People are afraid to come ere'. They say de ground ere' is cursed." Molly whispers cryptically. "They think that you'll get the wastin' sickness if you come ere'."

Well, she is partially right. Large funerals were held at these richly decorated marble monoliths. That was the best way for disease to spread. People would pack in around the grave straining to hear what beautiful things the minister had to say about the recently departed, all the while spreading the airborne virus that caused the wasting disease. They came here to mourn a death, and then, unwittingly bring it home with them.

"T 'would make a brilliant campfire story." Mollie said.

"Or a crime in real life," I add.

Mollie chuckles, her face brightening a bit. "Sure would!" She agrees.

I look around the darkness; it really makes these tombs look more frightening and forbidding. They seem to be closing in on us. I can see movements in the shadows. It makes me very nervous, so I take Mollie by the arm.

"Let's get out of here." I whisper harshly.

Mollie nods. "Tis' not a place to be lingerin in the darkness," she says in a frightening voice.

Chapter 18

Ian

I pull the cart carrying Lucie down through the oldest part of the cemetery. Mollie and Jess are coming in from the mausoleums where the rich people are buried, where my parents are buried. I remember how all the government officials wore isolation suits and re-breathers, so they would not be infected by the sick that attended the funeral. They were only there out of necessity, for show; trying to get the 'common man' vote after my father had fallen victim to the 'plague' as they called it. Even in the throes of the plague, they were politicking. There were even fewer people at my mother's funeral, and then just Jess, Lucie, and I when we buried my brother. It all seems so surreal, being out here again.

Many of the graves surrounding me are from the 1800's, and the gravestones here were just weathered marble crosses or cast iron crosses with names in foreign languages on them. Some are so weathered that there were no names on them at all. They were those who came before all of this, the settlers who actually built what had become a thriving city, and then crumbled to the gang infested mess it currently is. I wonder if they ever knew what would come of the world they were creating. What they would think of the jumbled mess we had made of their beautiful idea. Did they even imagine the giant buildings that would grow from their farmer's fields, or the innovations that came from their hand-hewn tools?

We studied the founders of our city in school it was mandatory. I went to a private school where all the students wore uniforms, and spent the day staring down their noses at each other. Yeah, I really fit in there. I am glad that Lucie never experienced the teasing and fake people there. None of them would ever imagine lifting a hand to grow their own food, or even building a wagon, like the one I pull behind me. They never knew what it was to struggle. I wonder what had happened to them. Are they still alive?

I am glad I am able to teach Lucie about the world. Teaching her the world as I see it. Not the fabricated world we had lived in before the wasting sickness. I kept all of my schoolbooks; they were my friends when I was shunned at my private school. I lived in the world of books; stories and facts that I could hold onto, even when I was falling apart.

Standing here, I can imagine the voices of those, who had gone before, whispering to me as I pass through their eternal resting place. It is almost like communing with old friends. I can only could take a moment's pause here, because I know if I stopped for a long time, I will be seen. This would mean certain death for both Lucie and I. The thought that we would become victims, and that our bodies would never be found sends a creepy feeling through my body.

The cart shifts a bit and I look back, thinking maybe Lucie moved in her sleep. I force myself onward to protect my family. Jess, Mollie, and Lucie are my world now. I will protect them with my dying breath.

Jess wanted to say goodbye to Justilian so we felt it fitting to meet there. We'd put him in the section where the city's founders were We had decided on this place because he was a founder of sorts. He founded a new way to help the people of the city, and to take care of the survivors that are left. In our own way, we were settlers too; our world changed so much in such a short period, like the settlers that came here changing their lives to build a new one. Justilian's body and spirit belongs with these brave people. He was one of the bravest people I knew.

I pause for a moment to catch my breath, and I look for Justilian's marker. I can see it from where I am standing. The small pile of white stones show up in the darkness, calling to me like a beacon. I get there first, because I am the closest. I only hope that Jess and Mollie are well on their way here. This definitely is not a place I want to stay for a very long time. Each minute that ticks by is a minute more my safety and the safety of my family is ebbing away. I hope Justilian's spirit is guiding us, and protecting us. Maybe, he will bring the spirits of these settlers to protect us as we travel through the cemetery.

    I stop at Justilian's grave and look down. The ground was sunken down a bit, as did many of the graves that were dug by families, who buried their loves ones. They did not have the help of the death dealers, and could not pay the exorbitant expenses for a funeral with a coffin, vault, or fancy decorated headstone. These are not the graves of the rich. They are makeshift graves, which sunk as the bodies degraded beneath the earth.

    "Ashes to ashes," I murmur, remembering the preacher's words at my father's funeral. "Dust to dust."

Chapter 19

Jess

There is a lot of overgrowth on the mausoleums from families who planted everything from small plants to fruit trees on the graves of their loved ones. Some of the trees they planted still bore fruit, but it would not be safe. The ground here was fouled. Beneath beautiful remembrances the rich families built to honor their loved ones, are mass graves. Many people do not know about the place where bodies of the poor are buried. They were buried by the starving, who were looking for a little money to buy food for their families. My mother was one of those people trying to provide for my brother, sister, and I.

Famine brought on the illness sooner, the wasting disease taking people emaciated by hunger and dehydration. These were easy targets for the sickness. It was as if death stood above the tenements wielding his frightening sickle above us, and we were condemned to die there. They compared the tenements in the news, to the death camps run by the Nazis. Although, this time they deemed acceptable, because the people sequestered there were already sick and dying.

A sharp crack catches my attention. I think I see movement in the darkness all around us; maybe even a flash of white, it keeps me on edge. All of my emotions are heightened lately, and it does not help that I am sick what seems like all of the time. Mollie has been amazing though, she really helped me get through it with herbal remedies while we were packing everything and moving it from one apartment to the next. It had been hell moving all of those items through the tiny passage we created in the dead of night while trying to keep silent. Several times, we stopped to widen the hole to bring the larger things through. Ian was cursing the entire time, and I had to hide my smile, or stifle a laugh every time he complained.

There is a muted shuffling behind us. I pause, holding the handles of the wagon, while looking around shifting my gaze quickly, hoping the offending individual will appear. I wipe my clammy palms on my pant legs, while the rough denim cleans at least a layer of dead skin off them. I look at them as they glow eerily in the dim moonlight. I was stupid not to have thought to wear gloves.

"Jess, ya all right?" Mollie asks her voice filled with concern.

"I thought I saw something. I think my eyes are playing tricks on me. It's too dark." I answer quietly.

"I can feel eyes on me as well." She agrees. "We need to be cautious, now more than ever."

I look around again. There's been something or someone in the shadows, staying out of my sightline. I feel like I'm in a B rated horror movie. During the scene where the killer is advancing on the silly blonde having sex with her boyfriend. Then they watch a scary movie. The blonde shrieks every time she thought she sees something, he falls back out of sight, until he is ready to have his way with them. Then, the killer advances mercilessly.

"How much farder to J's grave?" Mollie asks in a hoarse whisper.

"About two more sections, if I'm right. It should take about ten minutes, if we move fast." I answer, not looking at her.

There is another crack. I take a sharp breath and freeze, waiting for another noise. Mollie's grip on my arm tightens. She is scared, which means something to me. Mollie does not scare easily.

"Let's get out of here." I whisper.

Mollie nods adding her other hand on the handle of the wagon, which relieves some of the weight on my body. It is hard to pull this with the way I feel. I don't understand what's wrong. I can't risk both Mollie's and my life by being bullheaded and not accepting her help. I know I need it. The danger is very real here and we are not going to tempt fate.

Chapter 20

Ian

I scan the darkness around Justilian's grave for any sign of movement, becoming even tenser with every second that passes. There's no sign of Jess and Mollie, and that worries me to no end. They should be here by now. I pray silently that they haven't been caught and worse yet, killed. I keep hearing noises in the darkness, which is adding to my nervousness. I grab the baseball bat I hid in my wagon. At least if I'm attacked, I will do some damage to my attackers and hopefully giving Lucie time to get away. I hope that if anything happens to us, Ash will find Lucie, and take care of her.

There is another loud *crack* in the distance.

"Who's there?" I yell, lifting the bat over my head ready to advance.

"Damnit! Ian you'll wake the dead!" Mollie curses.

"I thought you were the Zombies coming to get us!" I yell breathing hard, while my heart races with the instant adrenaline rush.

"And what were you going to do, challenge them to a home run contest?" Jess teases, pointing to the bat on my shoulder.

"Hey, my dad always kept a bat by the door." I said, "Just in case."

"Whatever floats your boat." Jess says, pulling a makeshift bow out of her wagon that looks deadly, but I wonder if it really works. "Just in case…" She continues smirking.

I throw her a look and replace the bat in my wagon, checking on Lucie in the process. She is still sound asleep.

Our nanny once told me, "that girl can sleep through world war three. I am relieved that she's able to sleep through all of this.

"We'd best get outta here." Mollie suggests, "I don't like it, s 'too quiet."

I help Jess load some of the heavier items from her cart to mine. We were extremely careful, and loaded our carts evenly; so as not to draw too much attention to ourselves. Now with her cart being the lighter of the two, we will be able to move more efficiently through the cemetery. The sooner we are all out of the graveyard, the better and safer we will be. We have no idea when that will be. As far as I know, no one has ever been to the other end of the cemetery. For all I know, there may not be one. It runs from city to city, while the sections act like roadways. It almost reminds me of a labyrinth.

"Jess let's go!" I whisper.

"What is it?" She asks suddenly very alert.

"I thought I saw something!" I whisper.

Jess grabs Mollie's hand, so hard Mollie cries out. Then, she breaks into a full sprint, while dragging Mollie behind her and dodging through headstones. Suggestion: I quickly follow them, while praying the wagons don't crash into a headstone. It wouldn't be good because the headstones would probably break into a million pieces.

There are so many graves surrounding us. I am unsure if we are running in circles, or if we are headed back to the city. For all I know, we are headed right into the Zombies' lair.

It felt like we were running for hours with the wagons bouncing precariously behind us. I look to my right and see that Jess collapsed to the ground heaving throwing up what little food she'd eaten. Instantly, I'm at her side, rubbing her back and whispering soothing words into her ear. I take a bottle out of my jacket, and offer her some water.

"No." She chokes retching again.

"What is it?" I ask panicking.

"I don't know." She breathes.

I feel her forehead. It's cool to the touch. "No fever that's good."

"Maybe, I have the flu, or mono, or something like that." She coughs.

Mollie moves into view. "Or maybe you're pregnant."

"What?" She asks, "Are you crazy?"

"When was your last cycle?" Mollie asks.

Jess stops I can see her counting through the days on her fingers. She looks at Mollie anxiously.

"It can't be!" Jess says in a hoarse whisper.

"Is it true?" I ask.

"I'm not sure? I mean I can't take a test or anything, but maybe." She says, not believing it herself.

I help her to her feet. "Are you okay? Do you need to rest?"

"Don't treat me as if I'm glass!" She yells, pushing me away angrily.

Again, I offer her some water. This time Jess accepts it gratefully.

"We need to go!" Mollie urges. "We can't stay here."

Jess grabs the handles of the wagon again.

"Are you sure you can go on?" I ask.

"Yes I'm okay!" Jess answers in frustration.

Mollie takes one side of the wagon's handles. "Let me help, please?"

"Okay." She whispers. Jess is a very proud woman, and she doesn't accept help easily.

There is another sharp ***crack*** I spin around and shove Jess behind me.

"Show yourself!" I order.

I can feel eyes on me. Dark figures appear and move towards us.

"Mollie!" I hiss.

She raises her staff, and circles it in the air.

"Lucie get down!" I whisper.

Jess retrieves her bow, and within seconds, she has an arrow knocked and ready to fly at the interlopers, who are coming at us quickly from all sides.

All of the sudden, I am hit in the face with a flashlight.

"What in the hell are you thinking? You shouldn't be out here in the Graveyard at night!" Bullitt growls angrily looking us up and down. "The boss is livid that y'all are gone!"

"We had to; the Zombies are patrolling our building." Jess explains. "It wasn't safe."

"Where the hell do you think you're goin?" He asks.

"The Promised Land!" Lucy pipes up excitedly.

"Oh, that fairytale again." He huffs.

"Look, you may not believe it, but we're at least gonna try to get there!" I point out angrily.

"You're gonna get killed." Bullitt mumbles.

"Cool your jets." Ash says coolly coming into view. "What in the hell are you doing out here?"

"Goin' to the 'Promised Land', the land of milk and honey." Bullitt answers sarcastically.

"I kinda thought you might leave." Ash says. "So, I've been doggin ya through the cemetery."

"Why did you choose now to show yourselves?" Jess asks angrily.

"You tore right through the edge of our camp." Ash answers simply. "We had to make sure you weren't the Zombies."

"Whatever." I say sarcastically.

"Boss.. boss…we found em! Can I have my way with her this time? Like ya's did at that Jess bitch's apartment?" Dagger puffs running up to Ash. He suddenly realized where he is, and who he's standing in front of.

"S…" he murmurs seeing Ash throw him a look that could kill.

"Have his way with me…" Jess seethes. "It was you!"

"Jess, I had to." Ash flounders. "It was that or lose my gang."

"Get the hell away from her!" I yell, grabbing the bat from my cart. I start walking toward Ash circling the bat in the air.

Bullitt steps in the way, and I bounce off his massive chest. He catches my bat in his huge hand.

"Stop!" Ash yells angrily. "Let them go!"

"Get the hell out of here!" I scream back at him.

Dagger and Bulitt look at Ash with confused faces. He nods and they are gone.

After several seconds of restraining myself from going after them, I realize Jess is gone.

"Mollie, where's Jess?" I ask panicked.

"I don't know lad." She answers shaking her head. "Find her, I'll stay with Lucie!"

It took me a while to find Jess. I found her standing at the edge of the section, staring into space. I can hear her shaky breathing.

I walk in front of her and look into her eyes.

"Jess?" I ask.

She doesn't move or acknowledge my presence.

"Jess, come on." I say calmly, taking her hand, trying to lead her back. Being here alone was dangerous. I was sure Ash and his goons were still hanging out in the shadows protecting us, but I was still unnerved by the silence. I try again to lead Jess. This time she offers no resistance, and follows me silently.

Chapter 21

Ian

When we got back, Mollie was standing protectively over my wagon, still holding her staff up ready to attack. Lucie's eyes glitter from under the tarp. I can hear her shallow breathing.

"It's okay Luce." I say, gently touching the lump that is her head and rubbing it gently. I feel her draw in a huge breath.

Jess was still standing a few yards off, processing what had happened. It all comes together in her mind, and hits her like a cement truck. I can see the gears turning in her head. Ash was the one who beat her. He had his cronies hold her down, while he raped her. She just faced that realization, and now she feels lost. I want to call out to her, to go to her, and take her in my arms. I want to tell her she is okay; and take all her pain away, so she won't be torn apart. I want to erase that night from her memory forever. I feel so powerless, so helpless.

"Ian." Mollie murmurs, tapping a pile of bags next to the wheel of the cart with her foot.

I turn and look down, there are several knapsacks probably filled with supplies left there. I want to leave them there. I know we should leave them, or better yet, make a fire out of them. We could burn them, while we dance naked in the moonlight. I know we can't do that because we need them, as much as I hate to admit.

Slowly I go through them, and pack the items into the carts. I'm keeping a careful eye on Jess, hoping she doesn't do anything crazy. I don't care how long it takes, I will give her the time she needs to pull herself together. To put on that strong face I know hides the pain inside. If we have to stay here all night, that is what we will do.

As I am removing bags from the pile, I see a small pink bag. When I open it, it's full of candy, there is also a white stuffed bunny. Ash never forgets Lucie, and I don't think he ever will. I'd been watching the shadows for any movement indicating that Ash was out there, but so far, I hadn't seen anything. I'll have to watch and wait. The sun, or what we can see of it, is coming up. That means a measure of safety we didn't have at night. We'll be able to see any attackers coming. I hope we can find our way out of here, and fast. I don't know which direction to go. I don't even know if any direction is going to take us out of here.

"Ian." Jess whispers, suddenly beside me.

I stand up, and take her hands. "Are you okay?"

"I don't know. I don't know if I'll ever be okay." She whispers.

"Jess, no matter what happens…" I began.

"I know." She says cutting me off, and looking deep into my eyes. It's like she is seeing into my soul.

She knew what I am going to say before I even think it. She always has. We're like two halves of a whole, a yin, and yang completing each other. I don't know why it took me so long to see it with Jess. Maybe, it is the sickness, the attack, or fleeing the city that clouded my thoughts. What I do know is we were brought together for a reason, and that we are stronger together.

I feel her head on my shoulder. Her body starts shaking with sobs. She screams and falls to the ground pounding on it ineffectively with her fists. I kneel down beside her.

"Easy Jess," I whisper, rubbing her back, shushing her, and rocking her back and forth. It is a feeble attempt at trying to soothe her damaged soul, but it is all I can do.

"Ian, I need you." She cries, pulling away from me and intensely looking at me with a tearstained face.

"What?" I ask, looking at her confused.

"I need you." She says again, her voice stronger now.

"You have me." I answer huskily, while resting my head against hers. "Now, forever, and always."

"No! I NEED YOU!" She says shakily, her hands ineffectively pulling me toward her.

I tilt her face upward, so I can look into her eyes. She looks at me with such innocence it tears at my soul. I kiss her gently her lips are barely beneath mine. I pull her closer. I can smell her heady scent, not floral, not fruity, just a scent that is uniquely Jess.

I pull her to her feet and pick her up, while cradling her in my arms. I don't take my gaze away from her. I look over at Mollie who is building a small fire to cook on, with Lucie chattering away beside her. I carry Jess farther into the graveyard where they can't see or hear us. I know this is a mortal sin. I don't care.

Chapter 22

Jess

I lay in Ian's arms, feeling complete for the first time in a long time. I don't know what has moved me to do this. He is so gentle, kind, and understanding. Now, he idly trailed his fingers up and down my spine, which is sending a pleasant tingle through my body. I look up at Ian, and his eyes are closed. When he feels me move, he opens his eyes and looks down at me.

"Are you okay?" He asks.

"Yes." I whispered.

"You're crying."

"Am I?" I ask touching my face. It's wet. I quickly wipe the tears from my face.

"Why now, Jess?" Ian asks with a puzzled look on his face.

"I don't know. Ian, I love you." I answer, my voice taking on a plaintive tone. "Are you angry?"

"No... Just confused." He answers flatly.

"About what?" I ask, suddenly feeling very guilty.

"We were almost killed last night, and then after you got angry at Ash, you decided that it was the right time for our 'first time'." He said. "I feel like this was to get out all that anger, to hide behind sex."

I didn't know what to say. I don't know why I wanted Ian last night. I knew the 'first time' is supposed to be special, but ours was more primal.

"Jess?"

"Ian, I-I just don't know. I've loved you for so long and now…"

Ian sits up taking my hands in his, while looking into my eyes, "I just don't want you to regret this."

I shake my head quickly from side to side. "No, Ian I don't regret anything with you. Not at all, I couldn't…I wouldn't."

"Jess…Ian?" Lucie calls out.

Ian looks at me and I nod.

"We'll be right there." He calls.

"Jess, I love you too." He murmurs. "But, we can't do this again. Not until we're safe. When we're sure we're going to survive."

I don't know what to do with that. He gets up and dresses quickly, leaving me alone.

I sob quietly into my knees. I don't care who hears me. I let out the pain and agony that has been tearing at my heart for months. I pound the ground beneath me, my hands aching with pain. I want the ground to crumble beneath me, to swallow me whole, and take me to Hell where I belong.

I didn't cry like this when my family died. I couldn't. I had to be the rock for everyone, including Ian and Lucie. After I was raped, I became an emotional wreck. Then, add the possibility of being pregnant, I'm a total emotional shit storm. I feel safe with my family. That feeling of safety could be my downfall. Something could happen to them, because I'm so emotional, and it would be my fault.

My thoughts turn to Ian. Did he hear me bawling? Was he not coming for a reason? Was he afraid I would seduce him again? Was he angry that I can be carrying Ash's baby? I begin to sob even harder, my tears fall bitterly down my face. The person who told me that tears are healing lied. Nothing could heal this terrible dark feeling I have inside.

Ian is going to hate me forever, and it is all my fault. He'll never forgive me for taking advantage of a bad situation. I can't believe I seduced him, so I could feel better.

I am sure that is what he thinks, I used him, and my request was not out of the love I have for him, but for a primal need. I don't know how to tell him that it was so much more. He needs to know, perhaps then he would not be angry anymore.

"Jess!" This time it's Lucie calling, and she sounds worried.

I get up slowly, my body aching. I put on my clothes, and steady myself against a headstone. Once more, my stomach rebels. I double over throwing up what food I have in my stomach. It hurts so much. I don't know how my mother dealt with this when she was pregnant. It is agony! I never learned about this in school.

Out of the blue, I feel hands on my back. They started rubbing it the way my mother did when I was sick. The warmth is very soothing. It takes several minutes for me to be able to stand again. When I look up, I see Mollie looking at me sympathetically.

"Are ya all right?" She asks.

"Yeah" I pant feeling as if any moment I would start heaving again.

"Let's get back to the fire, I've got some ginger. We'll make a tea to get ya feelin' right."

"Thanks Mollie." I cough, wiping my mouth on my sleeve. "Where's Ian?"

"Down there, he's actin' weird. Very quiet, not his normal self." She answers.

"Yeah, well that's my fault." I mutter.

"Sex can do that, 'specially for the first time between 'friends'." Mollie surmises. "Tis' not something to take lightly." She continues solemnly.

"I know." I agree, as tears flow down my cheeks. "He's angry."

"No 'es not." She answers quickly. "He kept lookin' up here, wantin' to be with ya. Worryin' about ya."

"But, he didn't come." I choke. "He didn't want to."

"Aww child, you'll figure this out. With a love like yours, it always works out." She says. "Tis' also very hard to figure out what kind of a love it is!"

"Mollie?" I ask completely confused.

She smiles at me warmly. Then, takes my hands and begins rubbing them. The friction takes the chill away from my fingers.

"Were you ever in love?" I ask.

"My sweet love was more like puppy love compared to yours. Yours is a forever burning fiery kind of love." She answers simply, and then walks down the hill to the fire.

Chapter 23

Ian

The rest of the morning is spent trying to avoid each other. I am still processing what Jess and I did. It was my first time, and I wonder if this was Jess' first time, not counting the rape. It will never be counted as a "time." I want to believe it was. I see Jess looking at me over the fire, her eyes searching for some kind of reaction from me. I turn away. I'm not ready to face her, not yet. My best friend, Thomas Anderson, had once told me that sex changes everything in a relationship. I laughed it off, because he was gay. Now, I understood the wisdom of his words.

Thomas Anderson was my best and only friend in that hellhole of a private school my parents sent me to. He joked that his parents sent him there to "reform" him. He said he knew more "reform students" now, than ever before. Was homosexuality really a reason parents would send their kids to private school?

When I started at the academy, I had no idea what it was going to be like. I'm standing in the foyer, and here comes Tom walking confidently up to me extending his hand.

"Hi, my name is Thomas Anderson, and I'm gay." He said.

Tentatively, I shook his hand completely slack jawed.

"So, now that we've gotten the awkward hello out of the way, welcome to the hole." He said laughing.

"Ian, nice to meet you," I said, smiling back at him. "Do you always greet new students this way?"

"Only the cute ones," he answered, winking at me.

"I'm straight you know." I said, quietly.

I thought he would pee his pants with as hard as he laughed at my comment. "I know."

"How?" I asked.

"Only a straight kid would wear those awful white sneakers with fancy black dress pants!" He said, trying to contain himself.

I looked down at my shoes, and then over at his. Of course, he was wearing Armani loafers.

I steal a quick look at Jess and wonder what Tom would think of her. As if she knows I am looking, she meets my gaze. "Damnit! Stop looking at her!" I yell at myself.

I turn away quickly, and start to slam stuff back into my backpack. Suddenly, Mollie appears beside me with a cup of hot tea in her hand.

" Ya' might need this lad," she says, kindly extending the cup to me. "It'll take the edge off yer pain."

"Pain doesn't describe it." I say bitterly.

"Do ya want to talk?" She asks, gently putting a hand on mine.

"No, we need to get out of here." I answered emptily.

It is not a lie. We need to move quickly, while we can still see where we we're going, and what is around us. It will be easier to make a straight path when it is light out.

"Lad, I know someone else that's hurtin' too." Mollie said, pointing over to Jess. "She thinks ya hate her, and ya never want anything to do with her again."

"I don't..." I begin, loudly, but then lower my voice to a rough whisper. "I don't hate her. I just…well, I just don't know how I feel right now."

Mollie nods in understanding.

As I watch her go, I can hear Thomas' voice in the back of my head. "Sex Changes everything."

Chapter 24

Jess

We walk for a long time in silence. The only time anyone speaks is to suggest a direction or read a headstone. Mollie has a certain knack for finding ones with strange Irish names on them, as she runs her hand over the faces of the weathered marble. She keeps telling strange stories about the meanings of the names. I know she is trying to warm the chill in the air that hangs between Ian and I, but it isn't working very well. Lucie is paying very close attention, and writing down names in her notebook as we slowly make our way from section to section.

"Lucie, what are you doing?" I finally ask.

"I thought, maybe, if we made new friends where we are going, I will help them find their families." She answers simply.

I smile at her and ruffle her hair. "How do you know all of them will be Irish?" I ask.

"Well, Mollie told me that Ireland is full of potato farmers, and where we're going has farms and farmers. So, maybe some of the people are Irish." She explains.

I quickly put my hand over my mouth to stifle my laugh.

"Lass, that's a heart of gold ye have." Mollie says from behind us.

Lucie smiles wide, and I fall back next to Mollie who is pulling the other cart. She gave me a break "for the wee babe," she said.

"My turn," I suggest, attempting to take the handles from her. She does not resist and lets them go, while keeping one hand on the outside of the right handle as a guide.

"Have ya talked to him yet?" She asks.

"No." I answer bitterly. "He won't even look at me."

"He will." She says, touching my hand with hers. The warmth is unusually comforting. She has a special magic that way.

"I wish he would hurry up. I don't know if he's angry with me, or not." I sigh, shaking my head.

"I think he's just confused, that's all." Mollie explains sympathetically.

"Maybe…" I agree.

We walk for a few minutes more in silence.

"Jess," Mollie says quietly.

"Yeah," I answer.

"Why did ya choose to sleep with him?" She asks timidly.

I drew in a deep breath. "I don't know." I whisper. "It just felt…right. Like an itch I needed to scratch, and the only one who could do that was Ian."

"How do ya feel now?"

"I don't know, a part of me feels fulfilled…at peace." I explain. "Then, there's this other part of me that's terrified."

"You'll find yer way." Mollie says reassuringly. "If yer stars are aligned."

"Mollie, you always speak in riddles." I retort exasperated, and amused.

"I'm Irish," she explains simply, laughing at her own joke. "I was born with a poetic tongue."

Chapter 25

Ian

It's good to hear Jess laugh, and to see her smile. She hasn't been doing much of that lately. I know I'm not helping matters. I haven't talked to her, since we left the campsite. That was several hours ago. I know I have to eventually, because it's inevitable. For now, I am happy navigating through the many sections of the cemetery. As long as the city was getting farther away, I know we are headed in the right direction.

Lucie finally chattered her way to sleep, so I don't have to listen to her ask why I'm mad at Jess. It takes everything I have not to snap at her and say; "Shut up." The weight of what I did is my cross to bear. I love Jess, but physical love, well I don't know if I was ready for that yet. Still we did it, and now I feel guilty. The road turns off and circles around a giant mound, which has plaques with names of military service people on them. I read each one carefully, and find that there is one for each branch. In the middle of the mound is a tall flagpole with a weathered and faded American flag on top of it. I know the names of those service members are not the ones who died evacuating my family, and they were from wars fought long ago. I said a silent prayer for those lost souls. Mollie and Jess are coming behind me, I chose to walk faster to scout the area, and to be away from Jess. It isn't long before I hear the crunch of the gravel under the wheels of the other cart, and the murmured conversations between Jess and Mollie. They fall into a silent reverence as they come into view, seeing this lonely lost treasure of times long ago.

"I wish we could go back." Jess murmurs, bending down to trace her hand along the plaques.

"What?" I ask.

"Nothing," Jess whispers, looking away quickly.

I inhale deeply. This is killing me. "Let's stop here and rest." I suggest.

"Okay," Jess agrees, taking the cart handle from Mollie and putting them down on the ground.

Mollie sidles up to my cart and helps Lucie get out. She's been riding for a long time, and has been an amazing travel companion. She never complains or cries. She accepts everything that comes. My kid sister is something else.

"Mollie, would you mind watching Lucie for me, while Jess and I scout ahead?"

Mollie nods and smiles at me, "No problem lad, we'll do our business here, and get cleaned up."

I take Jess by the hand. She follows me gingerly. When I know we are out of earshot of both Mollie and Lucie, I turn to face Jess. She instinctively looks down at the ground. Gently, I lift her chin, so I can look directly into her eyes. I didn't notice the tears that were pouring down her cheeks. When I see them, I brush them away.

"I'm sorry." I whisper, choking back my own sob.

She stares at me, her eyes boring into my soul.

"I know I've been being a jerk. It's just that, I'm scared. I don't want sex to change the way you feel about me."

"It doesn't," she whispered.

"We can't be sure of that. I wanted our first time to be…special. I wanted it to really mean something to both of us. There are not any take backs; you cannot do your 'first time' again. I wanted it to be out of love, maybe, even after we had Mollie marry us. I just wanted it to be right, and now I feel like I've taken that from you and let you down; like a carnal, uncontrolled, animalistic, idiot."

"I wanted it, too." She chokes.

"I know, and I think we did it more out of desperation and fear." I answer, trying not to cry, not to raise my voice, and show my anguish over how everything happened.

"Maybe, we did." She breathes.

"It's so soon after…" I begin, but think better of my words. "Are you sure you're okay?"

"I'm all right." She whispers, as she leans into me, and sobs into my chest.

"I promise next time won't be so empty." I whisper into her hair. "I'll make it beautiful, and amazing. I promise you this from my heart and soul."

Chapter 26

Jess

My damned emotions have been running so high lately. I don't remember my mother being a completely blubbering, bawling mess when she was pregnant. Yet, here I am again bawling in Ian's arms like a big baby.

"Damnit," I think angrily, pulling away from him abruptly.

He looks at me stricken and confused.

"This isn't me!" I sniffled. "I'm stronger than this!"

"I know." He agrees, smiling at me, and trying to stifle a laugh.

"We're okay?" I ask tentatively.

"Yes," he answers thoughtfully. "You're going to keep your promise, right?"

"What promise?"

"No, sex until it's right." He says blushing.

"I'm not worried about me," I retort wickedly. "It's you that I should be concerned about!"

Suddenly, his lips are on mine astounding me with a soft, sweet, urgent kiss.

"Who are you worried about?" He murmurs giddily, raising his eyebrow.

"No fair." I mutter.

He grins at me.

"Do you know where we are?" I ask, looking around us, trying to change the subject.

"No clue," he answers "still in the graveyard."

I look at him "Duh."

He laughs. "Well, the city is still behind us, so we must be traveling in the right direction, and not going in circles like we thought a while back."

"I wish we had one of those maps, like my parents got at Arlington. It told us where everything was." I said. "I must have gone over it a thousand times planning where we would go, and we *still* got lost."

"That's what I brought these for." Ian said, producing a pair of binoculars.

"Cool!" I said, taking them from him. I am hoping to see anything but graves.

"They were my Dad's," Ian explains. "He liked to watch birds."

"Really," I asked.

"Yeah, kind of a genetic thing," he replies sheepishly.

"You like to watch birds?" I ask, surprised.

"Well, yeah." He answers, scraping his foot on the ground. "But, not really like my father. He could name all the types, breeds, and species of birds."

"Was he an ornithologist?" I asked, using the proper name I learned in school many years ago.

"Kind of," he answers quickly looking away. It frustrates me how he does that when we start talking about his family. He always shuts down until we change the subject. There is no sense in asking Lucie, she doesn't remember.

I put the binoculars to my eyes and start slowly turning around. I stop to giggle at the extreme close up I got of Ian's nose. He laughs and pushes me backwards. I continue to turn in the same direction. Then I see it, just a speck surrounded by graves, but not graves. It is something big, but I'm not too sure, what it is.

"Ian look," I exclaim, handing him the binoculars.

He takes them and looks in the direction I am pointing.

"What *is* that?" He murmurs.

"I don't know, but we're going there." I answer matter of factly.

"What if it's a trap?" he warns.

"If anyone is unfriendly there, we're bound to run into them sooner or later. I'd rather do it on my own terms." I answer with determination.

I take the binoculars from him and find it again. Then, I look at the top of the binoculars between the lenses.

"What are you doing?" Ian asked.

"There's a compass here." I explain. "Didn't you know that?"

"No. I just thought it was a decoration. I didn't know it really worked." He answers.

I mutter something like, 'typical guy' and note that we need to travel northwest to get there.

"I think it will be a couple of hours walk, if we don't stop." I surmised.

Ian sighs heavily, not completely agreeing with the plan, but he knows that he isn't going to shake my resolve. "Let's go then."

Chapter 27

Ian

Jess is crazy. She has decided to travel towards a speck that we have no clue what is. If that isn't bad enough, the speck is in unknown territory, in a place where we may or may not meet people who may or may not be friendly, and who would or would not possibly try to kill us.

No, that is not crazy. It is all kinds of *stupid*! I am not going to argue with her though. Jess is headstrong, overly brave, and occasionally reckless. That is what I love about her.

Jess frequently uses the binoculars to make sure we are traveling the right direction. With each step in that direction, my trepidation grows. I have a strange feeling that something is off about this whole situation. It is almost like a walking into the belly of the beast kind of feeling.

"Do you really want to do this?" I ask for the hundredth time.

Jess stops and turns to glare at me as best she can from between the wagon handles. Mollie almost falls down, because Jess stops so abruptly.

"Damnit Ian!" She curses.

"Well, I didn't do it!" I shot back.

"Ian," Jess says calmly. "We've been in their territory ever since we saw that speck. We might as well go there to show that we are being respectful, and to ask for safe passage. Maybe, they know the way out of here."

"I guess," I began.

"Ian, Jess is right. We need to do right by whoever claims these parts. If not, we'll look like a threat, and that'll mean danger for sure." Mollie agreed.

"I'll protect ya, Ian." Lucie pipes up. "Ash showed me how to knock knees!"

"He did?" I ask surprised. *Where was I when this happened?* I think to myself.

Jess stifles a laugh.

"All right, I guess I'll go along with this hare brained scheme, as long as Lucie will protect me." I concede sardonically.

Lucie sits back in the wagon looking very pleased with herself.

"Lead the way, oh mighty one." I say to Jess gesturing grandly.

Lucie giggles as Jess takes the lead, throwing a dirty look my way. I look up at the sky, and notice the light is fading. I hope we will make it there before darkness falls. The darkness here is very dangerous. This time we won't know who, or what is coming. I sure hope we made it to whatever it is, and whoever lives there is friendly. Otherwise, I am sure we are all as good as dead.

There is only one thing I do know, if we are walking into trouble, there is no one better than Jess to get into trouble with.

"Jess, what happened to your crossbow?" I ask nonchalantly, and a little sarcastically.

"It got broken when those guys attacked me. I couldn't fix it." She answered sadly, shaking her head, "And it was a real good one, too. I made that other bow, but it just doesn't work as well as my crossbow."

"Dang," I whisper. "Coulda used it."

"*Ya think?*" She answers sarcastically.

Chapter 28

Jess

Navigating the second leg of the graveyard is proving to be difficult. Mollie doesn't know where she is going any more, since she's only been as far as the Veteran's memorial. The object I saw in the binoculars is getting closer to us. It looks more and more like a house of some sort, and becomes more detailed each time I check. I'm going by sight alone, and following the direction on the compass.

"How much further?" Ian asked. "We're losing light."

"From what I can see, one section, maybe two?" I answer, looking through the binoculars. The outline of the top of the house has become completely clear. It has four different spires and an elongated sloping roof. Darkness and trees hide the rest of the house.

"If we move quickly, we could possibly be there in twenty minutes." I add.

"Well, what are we waitin' for?" Mollie said brightly. "A hot supper is in sight!"

"But, who's on the menu?" Ian mutters.

I shoot him a look, "Damnit, could you be any more negative?"

He sighs heavily, "Sorry."

I hear a loud snap to my right. I freeze and feel Mollie pull up beside me.

"Shh…" I hiss.

Lucie's eyes get very wide. You can hear her breath coming quick and shallow as the fear grips her.

"Breathe, Luce…" Ian said, reaching to rub her shoulder.

"Show yourself!" I demand loudly.

There is another snap. I can't see anything, it's too dark, and I don't dare get the flashlight from the back of my cart. I don't want to break the tight rank we instinctively formed. I can dimly see Ian's back and I am sure he could see mine. I don't want to leave him, Mollie, or Lucie exposed.

"Show yourself!" I demanded again, an unfamiliar growl creeps into my voice.

Slowly, three figures wearing black hooded sweatshirts appear out of the darkness. They're carrying ornate long bows; and they have their arrows trained on us. I back up a few paces, tightening our ranks even more.

"Lucie, get down from the cart very slowly." Ian whispers.

"Who are you?" I demand.

"We should ask the same of you." A girl's voice shoots back at us.

"We're not here lookin' for a fight." Mollie pipes up. "We're just passin' through here."

"Why would three kids and a runt want to travel through the graveyards, there's nothin' but death to those who try?" A boy's voice echoes over the tombstones.

"Then, at least we'll die free of the gang's oppression." Ian answers quickly.

I stare at him a moment, shocked at his words.

"So, it is freedom you're looking for?" The girl's voice asked, "a very dangerous endeavor. What if we wanted to enslave you ourselves?"

"We could take ya," Mollie said, sounding uncharacteristically vicious. "Just because I'm blind, doesn't mean I can't mix it up with the best of em'."

I am shocked at her behavior, we are not here looking for a fight, but it sure sounds to me like Mollie is.

"Yeah, I can fight too!" Lucie said, popping out from between us, ready to commit to this ill thought endeavor.

The girl starts to snicker, and then the two other boys join her.

"I'm serious!" Lucie squeaks.

"I know." The boy says through booming laughter. He lowers his hood, revealing that he had spiky brown hair and piercing green eyes.

The girl also lowers her hood. She is a short-haired brunette. She looks to be maybe sixteen or seventeen.

The other boy looks younger. He has close-cropped brown hair. It reminds me of the crew cuts they wore in the military.

"My name is Joshua." The green-eyed boy said. "This is Adam, and Malia."

I draw in a deep breath, while letting my guard down just a little. "I'm Jess. This is Mollie, Ian, and Lucie." I said, carefully pointing to each, as I say their name.

Joshua walks over and kneels down in front of Lucie. He reaches to tousle her hair. Ian instinctively moves to protect her.

"It's all right." Joshua said, smiling at Lucie warmly. "We mean you no harm."

"What're ya doin' way out here?" Mollie asked, placing a hand on Lucie's shoulder.

"Our parents ran this place." Malia explained.

"You're family?" Ian asked surprised.

"Far from," Joshua laughed standing up. "There were three different families of death dealers out here. " They could never keep up with the rising death toll from the plague. We're just friends who grew up together out here."

"Are there others?" I asked.

"Yes," Malia answered. "Jeff and Ashanti are back at the mortuary with Max."

"Mortuary," Ian gulped.

"Chill dude," Adam laughed. "There ain't been any bodies there in like forever."

"You look like you could use a hot meal." Adam said kindly.

"Sure could." Mollie said.

My stomach rumbles in agreement.

Malia laughed. "Then come on!" She said enthusiastically. "It's been ages since we've seen anyone out here."

Chapter 29

Ian

When Jess, Mollie, Lucie, and I get to the camp of the Grave Dwellers, four other members of their family greet us. There is Angel, a pretty, blonde haired, blue-eyed girl whose name matched her looks, August a tall skinny boy with olive skin and dark eyes, and Maggie a redheaded spitfire who Mollie hits it off with immediately because they look so very alike. The least imposing person is their tribal leader Max. He is tall, skinny, and unusually well dressed. He wears thick pop bottle glasses that all, but obscured his hazel eyes. His jet-black hair is short and kept slicked back. We find out that Angel and Max are brother and sister.

Malia invites us to help her sister Ashanti prepare the stew we were going to eat for dinner. While we are working on preparing stew with Ashanti, we find out there are several other tribe members including Jeff and Adam, who happen to be brothers. It surprised me that they were helping us prepare the meal, mostly due to their scary looking spiky biker attire. Apparently, they were given women's work as a punishment for something, but they were too embarrassed to say what the infraction was. Only that Max was deeply offended. Mollie offers some of her root vegetables for the stew and Jeff eagerly goes with her to get them.

Max seems to gravitate and hover around Jess, questioning her about the changes in the city. Jess obliges him, and fills him in on what parts of the city are taken over by gangs, and which ones are safe for trade. She warns him of Ash's group who are located outside of the city. I feel a little jealous, and creeped out that Max is hanging around my girl.

The camp itself is settled outside an old mortuary building. The mortuary looks like a tall blue, broken down Victorian mansion to me. I wonder if it is the same mortuary that took care of my father and mother. I don't remember much about either of their funerals, because I had been sequestered in a room next to where my father's casket was. I was not allowed to lift the lid to look inside for fear of infection. The same happened when my mother died.

"Kinda gloomy isn't it?" Malia said shyly, coming up beside me and offering me a cup of steaming hot coffee.

"Yeah, I never liked these places much." I agreed.

"My mom and dad used to keep flowers in the gardens, so that there would be life surrounding a place where death seems to rule over everything." She said smiling at the memory. "They wanted to remind the living that life didn't stop once their loved one died."

"How can you stay here?" I ask incredulously. "With all the terrible things that happened, that you saw coming through here?"

"Because Ashanti is here, and this has always been our home." She answered simply. "It's the same for all of us. All we have left in the world is here."

"How do you survive out here?" I asked. "There's no one to trade with."

"Let me show you!" She answers, smiling at me, while her eyes twinkle.

She takes my hand leading me inside the huge mortuary building. Outside the building appears to be in such great disrepair, that I thought it might fall down, but the inside is kept immaculately. The mahogany woodwork is polished, and the marble floors are shiny. Even the beautiful Tiffany fixtures show no signs of dust.

"Max does this." Malia explains, smiling in amusement at my slack-jawed response. "He says it's to honor all those that passed through these doors."

"Amazing," I breathed.

Malia leads me upstairs to a glass enclosed room, which I guess is up in one of the four spires on the building. She turns on the light, and I gasp at the amazing garden that fills this room.

"How did you do that?" I say completely dumbfounded at the lushness of their garden. Sure I saw Mollie do it, but she only could do root vegetables in the small vacant lot beside her building. There were so many more plants here tomatoes, cucumbers, huge strawberries that Lucie would flip over!

"We grow all our own food here." She explains. "Each of the four towers has a garden in it. We've been trying to grow and mill wheat, too!"

"Who…how?"

"Max built the gardens, because the drainage in these rooms is perfect for it. These used to be the embalming suites. We don't get much natural light up here, so we use the medical lamps, but Max hopes one day the sun will come back."

I shudder at the thought of dead bodies lying in these rooms. I take a few steps back, and Malia giggles.

"I could talk to Max," she offered. "Maybe, you could stay here with us. It would be a great place to raise the baby."

I turn to her, surprised "How did you know?"

"I can tell she's showing a little." Malia said simply. "My mother was a midwife, I learned a lot from her. How far along is she?"

"Two, maybe three months. I'm not sure." I answer.

"Well, if you stay here, I can deliver the baby for her." Malia said enthusiastically.

"We can't stay here. We're on our way west to what most kids call The Promised Land." I explained. "We're just passing through."

"Oh…" She said sadly. "Is the baby yours?"

"No." I answer bitterly.

"Oh." She whispered. "I thought you two were lovers?"

"We are." I answered quietly. "How did you know?"

"I can see it in the way you look at each other, Malia said bashfully. "I hope one day Max will look at me like that."

"You love him?" I surmised, seeing the pout that has formed on her heart shaped face.

She nods shyly at me and a hint of a blush tinges her cheeks.

"Ever since we were little," she said. "He was like a brother to me, but after our parents died, we became a little closer. How did you meet Jess?"

"We lived on the same apartment block. We helped each other." I answered. "I hope to marry her one day."

"Have you asked her?" Malia said hopefully.

"No…not yet at least." I murmured.

"You should, I bet she would say yes."

"I don't know with everything that's happened to her recently." I say, trying to skirt the issue.

"No excuses, ask her!" Malia said stubbornly.

"When did you become an expert on love?" I shot back at her.

"It's common sense silly." She said. "I even know where you can get a ring."

We start walking back down the hallway with Malia in the lead. At the other end of the hallway, there is a big room. Off to the right of us, there is another staircase, which leads higher into the tower. I look up into the gloom in trepidation wondering what might be up there.

When I look back down, I realize Malia has disappeared.

"Malia?" I called.

She reappears with her hand extended to me, with her fingers closed over something. She prompts me to give her my hand, and then she slips something cold and hard into it. I open my palm to reveal a pretty, silver antique spoon ring.

"It's beautiful but…" I begin.

"Don't you worry; it isn't from anyone who was dead. Adam and Jeff make them." She explains, amused at the morbidity of my unspoken thoughts. "If she says yes, we can use the chapel here!" Malia suggests excitedly. "We need some happiness around here."

"Whoa…wait…"

"No excuses." Malia reminds me.

"All right," I sigh. There is no arguing with this girl.

We go outside and Malia grabs Jess, pushing her from behind towards me. As soon as Jess is smack in front of me, Malia disappears.

"So, what did you want to talk to me about?" She asks completely confused.

Great…I have not rehearsed this at all. "Let's take a walk."

She blushes, and takes my hand. I walk her around the other side of the mortuary where a beautiful garden must have once been. There is a pretty, white gazebo in the middle of it. I lead her to it and help her sit down on the railing, after checking to see if it is sturdy.

"Jess, I know our love is pretty new." I begin nervously. "But, I know you've loved me for a long time, and well…I know I've loved you since the first moment I laid eyes on you."

"I love you, too Ian." She said shyly. "You know that."

"Well, I thought maybe we could make things more permanent."

"What?" Jess asked.

"I mean, would you…will you…" I take the ring out of my pocket and get down on one knee, while holding it out to her. "I could love you, forever, Jess. Will you marry me?"

She is dumbstruck. She stands there staring at me as a mix of emotions flows over her face. I hold my breath.

"I knew this was a bad idea." I said, getting up. Before I could, she grabs my face and kisses me before I can say anything else.

"Of course, I'll marry you." She whispers, looking deep into my eyes.

Chapter 30

Jess

"He asked me to marry him. I can't believe it," is all that I can think as I stare down at the antique silver spoon ring that fits my finger perfectly. Laying here beside him by the fire with my hand on his chest, I can feel the steady and soothing beat of his heart; and it belongs to me.

We are met with thunderous applause when we came back to the fire. I think Malia had something to do with that. Lucie is thrilled and can't stop jumping up and down, and hugging me. I asked her to be my bridesmaid and she started crying. Mollie agrees to marry us first thing in the morning, and we accept the Grave Dwellers' offer to take care of everything else.

I look up at the sky and I can tell that morning is coming fast, but I'm too excited to sleep. My stomach is fluttering with a mixture of excitement, and nervousness. Ian's hand trails up and down my back, sending electric tingles through my body. He loves me, and he is all I need. I'd be happy if I died right here, right now. My future is so uncertain. I have no idea what changes the baby I am carrying will make in my life. It seems safe enough to have the baby here, but something in my gut tells me it's a bad idea. I worry that the Grave Dwellers are not who they seem to be. The entire small society seems too perfect, too welcoming. The fact that the mortuary is kept pristine is completely odd, since no one needs the death dealers anymore.

"Hey." Ian murmurs looking down at me. "You okay?"

"Yeah," I lie.

"You sure?" He asks, his eyes glittering in the darkness. "You're not getting cold feet are you?"

"No! Not at all!" I answer, curling closer to him.

"Then, what is it?" He asks, hugging me gently.

"The Grave Dwellers, you don't think there's something off about them?" I ask haltingly.

"No, however, the way Malia looks at you is a little creepy." He answers.

"What about that guy, Max? Don't you think he has some kind of ulterior motive with letting us be here?"

"Look Jess," Ian says, pulling himself up, so he can look into my eyes. "They have enough of everything that they're not going to want our stuff. Besides, we are right here. We can see, and hear anyone if they were to attack us."

"I know…" I begin.

"And Jess, I'll protect you. No one and I mean no one will hurt you as long as you live. I pledge this to you." He continues, with a hint of desperation in his voice. "We will leave this place if it makes you happy. We are starting over together. You and I, Mollie and Lucie are a family. We protect each other."

I nod.

"Get some sleep, morning is going to be here before you know it. It is our wedding day. Focus on that." He says, stroking my hair trying to soothe me, trying to take away the fears that threaten to overtake me and send me running for my life.

"Sleep my beautiful Jess, a new life is starting for us. Full of hope, beauty, and amazing things." He croons in a soothing singsong voice. "I love you my beautiful Jess."

He starts humming my favorite hymn; I fall asleep listening to the steady baritone of his voice. "*Amazing grace, how sweet the sound…*"

Chapter 31

Ian

Jess sleeps fitfully, and I can't blame her. She has so much fear pent up inside of her. She hasn't even let me know what her thoughts are about the baby. It's a subject that is always left unspoken like its taboo. Jess has a solid exterior, but I know her heart. She has a way of knowing things that are going on inside of people. She knows their character, so I have to trust her that the Grave Dwellers are hiding something from us. The sooner we get out of here the better.

"No…Nooo…" Jess moans turning her head from side to side as tears spill down her cheeks.

I stroke her cheek, "shhhh it's all right, honey you're safe."

The dull red light is filtering through the dust and grime that has formed permanent smudges across the sky. I'm going to let her sleep as long as I can. Today is our wedding day. In a perfect world, Jess would walk down an aisle filled with gorgeous flowers, the heady aroma filling the air with the scent of innocent love. Her father would be dressed in a black tuxedo trying to hold back his own tears, as he gave away his little girl. I would be standing in the front of the church with Andy beside me as my best man. I would argue with my parents about the pretention of having anything but a simple wedding. My mother would be crying as Lucie walked down the aisle in a pretty dress carrying a tiny bouquet, which would be an exact replica of the one that Jess would be carrying. The organ would start to play the wedding march and then…

"Are you getting up?" Lucie complains hovering over me, and waking me from the dream wedding, I have created. Am I dreaming? Is any of this real?

"What is it stinky?" I grumble, closing my eyes.

"Duh…you're getting married today!" She snipes back.

"Would you be quiet please?" I hiss. "You're going to wake Jess. She needs to get her beauty sleep."

Lucie huffs something like "five more minutes" and stomps off.

I laugh to myself; my little sister always did things two hundred percent. I turn to wake Jess with a gentle kiss on her lips, and both of her cheeks. Her eyes flutter open and she looks up at me. Then smiles that sweet beautiful smile I've come to love. Gosh, she is so breathtakingly beautiful.

"Mornin," she sighs sleepily.

"Good morning to you." I murmur kissing her again.

"So, we're getting married." She sighs dreamily.

"Yep," I answer.

"I don't have a dress." She says flatly.

"I don't have a ring." I tease, winking at her.

"Some bride and groom we are." She giggles kissing me playfully.

"We better get up." I suggest. "Lucie is already freaking out."

"And that's different than any other day because…" Jess teases.

"Yeah, I know." I agree, stifling a laugh.

It does not take long for Malia to whisk Jess, Luce, and a cursing Mollie off to be beautified, once she discovers we are awake. I hang out by the fire checking, and re checking our gear. We will be leaving tomorrow, and if we have to run, I want to be ready.

"Ahem." I turn around as Max cleared his throat. He stands in front of me with a hanger covered in a garment bag that looks far too large, extended to me.

I look at him quizzically.

"Trust me, you will be underdressed." He says curtly, as I take the bag from him. Then, he turns and walks away briskly.

"Thanks," I mumble watching him go.

"Don't mind him." Adam says, coming over to me. "His parents were the same way, professional death dealers with no social skills whatsoever."

I laugh. "What's his deal anyway? He seems awfully freaky and nerdy to even be your leader."

"Max's parents were the last ones we lost. He insisted on dressing them up in funeral vestments, and even attempted to embalm them. They looked terrible, but it made him happy. Of course, they were cremated. He keeps their ashes in his room above one of the garden rooms. He stays up there and holds conversations with them. Sometimes, he makes Angel go up there with him, but she usually avoids him when he gets like that."

"That's completely morbid." I mutter without really realizing it. I look up at Adam apologetically.

"Hey, you're only voicing what everyone else thinks." Adam agrees, laughing at me.

Then, I look at the garment bag and gulp. Adam laughs even harder. "Don't worry, those are brand new, we have a huge closet of brand new stuff down in the basement. They used it for paupers' funerals, which are what Malia's parents dealt with mostly."

"Well that explains a lot." I said. "She's really great."

"Yeah, she is." Adam agrees wistfully.

"You like her?" I ask.

"Yeah, but she only has eyes for Max." He answers, disheartened. "Most of the girls here do."

"Max?" I ask, in disbelief. "Why?"

"Who knows," Adam said. "I mean, sometimes it's kind of creepy, like when he was hovering around Jess."

"Jess can hold her own," I said, smiling at the thought of Jess turning Max down flat. "Don't worry about Malia, she'll come around."

"Yeah, maybe; but right now she is a member of the cult of Max." He said with a hint of anger in his voice.

I leave it at that. I don't want to go any further into something that can get us all killed.

"Is there a place to change?" I asked, holding out the garment bag.

"Yeah, you can use the bathroom inside. The girls are all upstairs, so you should be safe enough from the beautification process." Adam answers, his mood brightening. "Come on, I'll show you."

I wonder what Jess thought when she walked inside, or if she was too rushed to take notice of how pristine it is in here. I'd described it to her but she really had to see it. Even the bathroom itself is spotless. I wonder if they ever use it. It even has the little complementary books of matches advertising the funeral parlor. I grab a handful of them and jam them in my pocket.

I use the mint scented hand soap to wash my hair, and give myself a sponge bath to take, at least, the first few layers of dirt and dust off myself. The suit fits perfectly, as if it had been tailor made for me. I shudder at the thought of Max tailoring this suit; it would be just like him to make this suit fit me perfectly, so that he could kill me and use it later. There is a red ascot in the bag, much like the one my father wore at the formal galas he and my mother attended. I am definitely not going to wear that. Instead, I opt for the black bow tie that looks a little too small that is in the same pocket as the ascot.

I look at myself in the mirror, and draw in a sharp breath. I had not realized until now how much I look like my father. His eyes are staring right back into mine. "I wish you were here." I think, as tears sting my eyes and fall unabashed down my cheeks.

Chapter 32

Jess

Malia fusses, frets, pokes, prods, preens, pins, curls, infuses, shaves, and plucks every surface of my entire body. Then, she rushes off to get the dress she wants me to wear at the wedding. I am happy to be clean, but it feels like the skin itching kind of clean, where you know you scrubbed your body raw.

Lucie looks adorable with her hair up in pigtails of curly ringlets. She wears a simple pretty, pink dress that Malia says belonged to her little sister. Malia raided the stock of fake flowers somewhere in the bowels of the mortuary, and put together two small bouquets of fake red roses, which smell a bit like mildew.

Molly looks regal dressed in her forest green velvet dress she carried with her from the city. Hear ears are adorned with beautiful emerald earrings that belonged to her mother. They match the stunning ornate, emerald cross she's wearing on her neck. I wonder about Mollie, I don't know that much about her, although, she had to be wealthy to have such beautiful clothes and jewelry.

Malia made Adam agree to be Mollie's guide dog for the day. It hadn't taken much persuasion at from her all, and I'm sure it's because Adam is sweet on Malia. Max hovered over Malia and Adam as they were discussing what his duties were. It was so creepy, and I swore Adam looked a bit angry and frustrated that Max was there.

"Jess…Jess! What do you think?" Lucie chants, grabbing my arms and showing me the pretty, pink clip on earrings Malia gave her to wear.

"She said I could have them! Aren't they beautiful?" She chitters excitedly.

"Shh…lass." Mollie says, calmly coming up behind Lucie. "Here, let me see." She says, opening her hand.

"Yes, very fine, very fine indeed." She coos, gently stoking the earrings with a feather light touch, "A real treasure!"

"I've got it!" Malia said, excitedly dancing into the room with an oversize garment bag.

"Oh my…" I breathe as she opens the bag, "Where did you get *that*?"

The dress is an ivory color with intricate beadwork that looks like tiny flowers all over the bodice. The dress is an A line cut, which is perfect for hiding my 'bump.' The bottom flares out ever so slightly and barely touches the ground.

"I made it." Malia says blushing. "This is my favorite one. My mother taught me to sew when we first moved here."

"Oh Malia, don't you want to save this for your wedding?" I ask, still in awe of the beautiful creation she is giving me.

"No, I'm going to wear my mother's dress. She even altered it before she died, so that it would fit me, a last gift." Malia explains shyly.

"Malia, thank you; I don't know what to say," I breathe, touching the fine lace that covers the skirt. "Thank you, so much. I love it."

Malia puts down the dress and hugs me. "It's my pleasure; it makes me happy to see you so happy."

"We'd best get ready." Mollie says quietly. "Ian's waiting."

I nod, quickly wiping away my tears.

"Let's get your face all fixed up." Malia says quickly wiping the tears from her face. "I've got all kinds of makeup."

"Ummm…" I begin looking a little bit mortified.

Malia smiles hugely and begins rummaging around in a large wooden box.

"Malia, ummm….." I say again, a little louder.

"Don't worry," she laughs. "We got rid of all the makeup they used on the bodies."

I breathe a guarded sigh of relief.

"Oh!" I say quickly. "My mother's cross necklace is still in a box in the cart."

"I know which one it is!" Lucie pipes up. "I'll be right back."

While Lucie is gone, Malia quickly does my makeup, touches up my hair, and helps me into my dress.

I can't breathe as I look in the mirror and see not a girl, but a woman looking back at me. She is so beautiful!

"One more thing!" Lucie sings, skipping into the room.

I carefully kneel down and allow her to clasp the necklace, so it rests below my hair and hangs over my heart. Lucie smiles as she looks up at me and produces my parents' Bible from behind her back.

"I thought you might need this." She whispers.

"Thank you Lucie," I choke kissing her forehead. A lump forms in my throat. This is the Bible my mother carried at her wedding, and the Bible her mother carried at hers.

"Hey," Adam says, appearing at the door. "Let's get this show on the road! Everyone's waiting in the chapel."

I nod as Lucie takes my hand leading me toward the staircase, and to my new life.

Chapter 33

Ian

I stand nervously in the chapel waiting for Jess to come in. Most of the Grave Dwellers are there sitting in the small rows of benches, speaking in hushed whispers. Jeff and Adam keep coming back and forth, whispering to Max who is standing at the back of the chapel. I'm not sure what that is all about. The only thing I know for sure is I want to marry Jess, and get out of here while the getting was good.

Ashanti moves to the small dark cherry upright piano that stands behind me, and begins to play what I think might have been a concerto. She plays it so beautifully, that it brings tears to my eyes. When I turn to watch her for a moment, I can see how lightly she touches the keyboard, her body moves with the rhythm of the music and gently sways back and forth.

Malia appears in the back doorway; Ashanti sees her and plays a cascade of gorgeous running notes into Canon in D, which was my mother's favorite song. Jeff and Adam close the back doors slowly. Max disappears completely, and I pray that he is not going to try to "give the bride away."

Malia is the first to come in walking slowly down the aisle in a much-practiced procession. She holds a bouquet of pretty, silk daisies. Her eyes shine, and she is smiling from ear to ear. I think I can see the glimmer of tears on her face. Then, she does something, which makes everyone in the room giggle. When she gets to the front of the chapel, she turns and runs back up the aisle, and out the back doors.

Adam opens the door and takes Mollie by the arm leading her regally down the aisle to the very front of the chapel, then turns her around gently. Then, he retreats to the back of the chapel. He closes his door again, and turns to wait for the signal for Lucie to come. There is an awkward pause as we wait for Lucie, who I am sure is going to come down the aisle any second looking nervous with her eyes locked on me. That is when she screams.

My heart jumps into my chest, as I run for the back of the chapel. I push Adam and Jeff out of the way, and tear the doors open. Jess is on the floor and Lucie is screaming and crying beside her. Max stands off in the shadows.

"He…He…stabbed her with something." Lucie sniffs; I can see she is terrified.

"What have you done?" I growl, looking at Max.

"Nothing, I was waiting to kiss the bride; for good luck." He answers sardonically.

I touch Jess' face gently. "Jess, honey wake up," I urge as tears fall from my eyes.

"He…used…this." Malia said, picking up an antiquated looking syringe. "Max, what have you done?" She gasps.

Jess' face is flushed, and she is sweating profusely. I leap at Max grabbing the syringe out of Malia's hands. I clench my fists around his collar and slam him against the wall. Jeff and Adam come running towards me, but Malia stopped them, she frantically whispers what Max had done.

"What was in here?" I growled shoving the needle in his face.

"Nothing that will kill her, I just want the baby." He seethes. "It's to be our next leader. I had a vision."

"A vision?" Malia gasps. "You had a vision that our child would lead."

"And ours." Ashanti says coming out of the chapel guiding Mollie to where Lucie sits on the floor shaking and sobbing.

"That was what he told me as well." Maggie adds, standing in the doorway flanked by August and Joshua.

Adam kneels down beside Jess, and picks her up. He carries her into the next room. Jeff leads Mollie, while August picks Lucie up gently in his arms trying to soothe her.

"Where are you taking them?" I yell.

"It's all right." Malia says, walking towards me. "There's a sofa in that room, Adam is taking Jess there."

"How can I trust you?" I seethe, slamming Max into the wall again.

"He lied to us all." Malia says in a plaintive tone. "What we don't know is why?" She said, looking at Max with an anguished look.

"Well, answer her!" I yell, shaking him like a rag doll.

"You are all too easy to manipulate." Max croons eerily. "If I gave each of you a child, you would all fight over who would rule here. The great angel came to me in my dreams, and said the outlander child would be my successor."

"What?" Angel said, coming up beside me and looks into her brother's eyes. "What of our child, the one that we made out of love. The blood of your blood."

"You got your sister pregnant?" I scream, feeling the blood pulse in my temples.

Malia pales, and backs into August, who catches her before she passed out.

"You're sick dude, sick." He says, looking disgusted, as he took Malia into the other room.

I feel a hand on my shoulder I shrug it off angrily. Then, it is there again more firmly. "Dude, let me take care of him." Joshua murmurs, in a very controlled voice.

I grab Max's collar tighter.

"I won't let him go." He says angrily. "I'm gonna lock him up until we decide what to do with him."

"No." I growled.

"Dude, Jess needs you." He urges.

It is true Jess needs me; but I need revenge, and that darkness is taking over my heart. I am filled with raging volcanic anger, and it's burning me from the inside out.

"What…did…you…give…her?" I spat, slamming Max against the wall with every word.

"Seco…barbital." He gasps, smiling at me crookedly. "It knocked her out but good."

"Why the hell would you use a surgical drug to knock her out?" Joshua breathes.

"Because…I…wanted…her…" Max chokes.

"Jess needs you." Joshua says again, squeezing my shoulder even tighter.

I push Max out of my grasp and he falls to the ground, hard. Joshua is on him before he can scramble away. I hear a sickening thud, and a crack, as I run into the anteroom where they took Jess. In seconds, I am kneeling beside the antique chaise where Jess lies motionless.

"It's all right lad." Mollie says, putting her hand on my shoulder. "She'll be all right."

I grab Mollie's hand and squeeze it. I begin to cry softly. The Grave Dwellers stand around us, looking at each other a mixture of confusion and shame on their faces.

"I'm sorry." Ashanti offers, "If we would have known…"

I look up at her and she backs away seeing the pain on my face. "How could you follow a sicko like this?"

"We didn't know." She answers quietly.

"Lad, let me stay ere' with Jess and Lucie. You need to take care of Max quickly." Mollie says.

She kneels down beside me and tries to help me up.

"I can't. I'll kill him." I breathe.

"No, ya won't." She says, gently squeezing my hand. "Ye know what ye ave' to do with im'. Death is too good for the sick bastard."

"Yeah," I agree, trying to fight the darkness taking over my soul. "You've got that right."

I struggle to my feet and slowly look each of the grave dwellers in the eye, one by one trying to read their minds. I'm hoping for some kind of tell as to what they are going to do next.

"What are you going to do with him?" I finally ask.

"He can't stay." Adam says flatly, sitting next to Malia, holding her hand.

"Yes, he should be banished." Ashanti agrees.

"Nooo!" Angel cries from the back of the room. "Look at all he built here, the gardens, the mortuary. We must be ready."

"Ready for what?" I spat at her, "the next Armageddon? Sweetheart, I have news for you, it isn't coming. All that cleaning, fixing, and polishing you've done. It is not worth anything. The death dealers are extinct. No one can afford them. The adults are gone, and your money is worthless. This place is as dead as the bodies that lay rotting in the graves around it!"

Angel steps back looking stung, and retreats into the hallway.

"You're right." Jeff whispers. "Their dreams were never our dreams."

"Let's get this over with." August says emotionlessly as he gets up and begins walking to the doorway.

I follow as the Grave Dwellers go into the foyer to tell Max his fate. Joshua stands over Max who is on the floor curled up in a ball. I see his glasses across the room broken in half, their lenses shattered. Angel is on her knees pleading with Joshua to let her brother go. She backs away as Jeff and Adam approach them.

"Stand up coward." Joshua orders dragging Max to his feet.

Max's nose looks clearly broken; it's bleeding profusely down the front of the crisp white shirt he has on under his suit. Both of his eyes are already turning black and bruised.

"Max, you've done the unthinkable. You've lied to us for too long, you attacked an innocent girl. You impregnated your sister. You can't stay here anymore." Adam states. "You'll be banished to the outlands under threat of death should you return here."

I look at Adam in shock. "The outlands…" I murmur.

"He did this to himself." Malia whispers her heart breaking. She walks over to Angel. "What of you sister, are you leaving too?"

Angel looks at Max, and then at the Grave Dwellers.

"She has to go, too." Jeff states mercilessly.

"She's pregnant." Malia pleads. "What of the child?"

"She can't stay." Adam agrees, coming over to turn Malia,

so he can look into her eyes. "They have to go, they hurt Jess. He would just come back here looking for her and the baby. It's not safe."

Malia starts to cry, Adam pulls her into his arms, whispering soothing words into her ear, and rocking her. "Baby, everything's going to be okay." He croons, softly into her ear.

Maggie appears carrying two backpacks. "I packed your things and some food." She says flatly.

Joshua grabs them with one of his huge hands, and then takes Max by the scruff of his neck with the other.

"Let's go." He growls.

Jeff grabs Angel roughly by the elbow. "We'll put them in the vault until we're ready to take them."

Joshua nods his agreement.

I follow the Grave Dwellers to the front of the building, and out the door. They follow a short path away from the mortuary, and we come to a cave containing some very old coffins. August comes forward to unlock the heavy metal gate blocking our way. Then, Joshua pushes Max inside. Jeff unceremoniously shoves Angel in there as well.

"How can I trust you'll do what you said?" I asked, not sure if any of these other people joined 'the cult of Max.'

Joshua comes to stand in front of me. "I promise you on the lives of my dead parents that justice will be done." He claps a hand on my shoulder and walks away.

Ashanti appears at my side and whispers. "He'll do it; Max and Angel are his brother and sister."

I stare at her in shock. She nods at me, and then follows the group inside. I hang back watching as Angel sobs over her injured brother.

"Why?" I ask.

"Because, the Dark Angel told me." Max rants then begins laughing manically as Angel sobs even harder.

Chapter 34

Ian

We spend the night inside the mortuary. Everyone feels safer knowing Max is locked outside. Even inside the thick walls, we can hear Max ranting and raving in the crypt. His laughter sends chills up my spine. Jess wakes up late that night, and we tell her all that has happened in the hours after Max attacked her.

Early in the morning, we watch as Jeff, Adam, and August take Max and Angel away. Joshua stays behind to make sure we are packed, and have enough supplies. He presents us with more provisions and some camping gear that he had stowed away in a footlocker down in the basement of the mortuary.

Mollie marries us with just the few Grave Dwellers as witnesses in a very simple ceremony standing outside by the fire.

She blesses our marriage with a Bible verse that comes from Genesis Chapter 2:

> *For wherever you go, I will go;*
> *and wherever you lodge, I will lodge;*
> *your people shall be my people,*
> *and your God, my God.*
> *Where you die, I will die,*
> *and there will I be buried.*

Jess is crying, and I kiss her tears away.

"You may now kiss dat' bride." Mollie announces proudly.

The Grave Dwellers clap as I dip a giggling Jess, and kiss her.

"Are you ready for our new life?" I asked her.

She smiles at me and blushes. "Yes, I really am," in a voice so innocent that I am taken aback for just a moment before I kiss her again.

Then, all of the sudden Lucie attacks us laughing, and crying at once. We all fall in a heap on the ground, much to the giddy enjoyment of the grave dwellers. Who begin laughing and clapping even harder than they already had been.

"Luce chill!" I complain.

"Nope! I'm too happy!" She laughs hugging us tight. "Now we're a really for real family!"

I look at Jess, and wink at her. "I guess we are." I agree.

"Yes." She says happily. "Let's get this new life started."

She stands up and offers me her hand. I take it and pull myself up and into her arms. At this moment in time, there is no better place to be.

Epilogue

Jess

We stay with the grave dwellers for a few days, so I can get my strength back. At least that's what Ian wants me to believe. I know it is because he wants to make sure that Jeff, Adam, and August would return without Max and Angel. Lucie sent a letter for Ash, just in case they run into him in the outlands, asking Ash to protect her friends.

Malia fusses over me finding different clothes I can use as the baby develops. I gladly accept them, because I have no idea what I am going to do when my clothes don't fit anymore.

I think about the baby more now, and how it will change my life. I'm more comfortable thinking about it knowing I'm not going to do this alone. I have Ian, Mollie, and Lucie to take care of me, and I know that they won't let anything hurt me, so long as we stick together.

The Grave Dwellers present us with "wedding gifts" of a cradle, and some baby items that Ashanti and Malia scrounged from who knows where. I don't even want to think about it. Joshua gives us a map he found showing the trails Max had taken on his *'spirit walks'* in the cemetery. While they were looking, they found the "Dark Angel" Max said he had the visions from in the tower where he and Angel stayed. It is nothing but a statuette of the Madonna that has been stored in the dark recesses of the attic. When they brought it down, it looked as if it had been through a fire, and was elegantly grotesque. Max cut a picture of his mother's face and taped to the front of the statue. Joshua and Ian took it out and buried it (and any evil that may have come with it) away from the mortuary, and the grave dwellers who need to start a new life without being under the evil thumb of Max. I wonder- what had happened to him to make his mind so twisted.

The morning we are ready to leave Adam, Jeff, and August return. They let us know that they ran into Ash, and that Max will be dealt with much to Ian's relief.

As for me, I feel safe for the first time in a long time. Ash sent back another bag of candy and toys for Lucie, and a letter for me. I put it in the box that holds my keepsakes. Maybe, I will open it one day. Today is not that day, I'm too happy. I don't want to relive all the anger and pain that Ash has caused me, not now at least.

"A penny for your thoughts?" Ian asks, coming up behind me, and wrapping his hands around my waist.

"Mmmm…nothing." I said, putting the box back in the cart.

He turns me around and kisses me gently on the lips. "You ready?"

"As I'll ever be." I answer.

"Then, let's go." He says, smiling at me and kissing me again very quickly. "I'll race ya!"

"We can take 'im lass." Mollie says, conspiratorially appearing beside me out of nowhere, and taking the other handle.

I nod and laugh, "Ready…Set…," then; I take off running, finally free from the darkness that has loomed over my soul for so long. My heart is happy, and I am ready for a new start.

Lee Ryder is a mother of three children and one angel. She currently lives in New England. At an early age, she began to write small works that were featured in local publications. She studied theater and vocal performance, and was featured in several musicals and plays. She believes in love at first sight, and married her soul mate at age 19. She also has read, reviewed, and edited other published works. You can visit her at her blog and on her on Facebook:

https://www.facebook.com/MsLeesFanfiction?ref=br_tf

http://leeryderabfa.blogspot.com/

Printed in Great Britain
by Amazon